Her Fantasy

LAUREN BIEL

Library of Congress Cataloging-in-Publication Data

Her Fantasy/Lauren Biel 1st ed.

Printed in the United States of America

Cover Design: Laura Hidalgo of Spellbinding Design

Content Editing: Sugar Free Editing

Interior Design: Sugar Free Editing

For more information on this book and the author, visit: www.Lauren Biel.com

Please visit LaurenBiel.com for a full list of content warnings.

This book is dedicated to all the women who love to collect book boyfriends who fulfill their deepest, darkest fantasies

Author's Note

This anthology-like novella will explore several different fantasies, kinks, and tropes, some of which are not safe for anyone with pearls to clutch. Make sure you check out Laurenbiel.com for a list of content warnings.

Chapter One

T he keys slipped from my hand and fell to the porch as I balanced the cumbersome grocery bags in my arms. "For fuck's sake," I said much too loudly for this quiet suburban neighborhood. I kicked the bottom of the door, and my husband opened it from the other side, his lips set tight.

"Why do you always try to bring them all in at once?" he asked.

"Take one trip or die trying," I said through clenched teeth, my arms tired and straining. That was a motto I lived by for most of my adult life.

After he relieved the burden of most of the bags, I picked up the keys and headed inside.

"You're so stubborn." He smirked at me as he placed the bags on the counter. I knew I was. I shaped my entire life around it.

I looked around the kitchen, which I kept immaculate at my own expense. If I wasn't working, I was cooking or cleaning. No one told me adulthood would be so repetitive and mundane. The sunlight gleamed off the white quartz countertops. Brown coffee stains glared at me from the counter by the coffee pot, and I fought the urge to clean them. I had more exciting things on my mind. I'd received an email telling me a long-awaited package had arrived that morning, but as I glanced around the kitchen, I didn't see it anywhere.

"Did I get a package, babe?"

Michael began pulling items from the bags and putting them away. "Yeah, I think it's still in the mailbox."

"Gee, thanks." I rolled my eyes as I trudged back outside and pulled the brown-paper box from the metal mailbox. My heart always raced a bit too fast when I got a new package, especially when it held something I was so excited about. I ripped open the top and pulled out five new paperback books, grazing my fingers over the spines as I went back inside and closed the door.

"Are those your smut novels?" Michael asked with a roll of his eyes.

"Damn right they are," I said as I spread them on the counter. The covers were magnificent. Each showcased dark themes with a gorgeous contrast of colors, and men were the centerpiece on each one—*delicious* men.

Michael leaned over and looked at them for a moment before curling his lip. He lifted one of the books, flipping it back and forth in his hand for a moment. He pulled his glasses from his breast pocket and perched them on his nose before silently reading the back. "A toxic, dark Cosa Nostra duet." He dropped it on the counter and pushed it away from him as if touching it had somehow soiled his fingers. "Why do you read this garbage, Zo?"

I hated when he called me Zo. That was the name he used when he thought I was being ridiculous. I was *not* being ridiculous. It was my hobby, and it made me happy. These books were art, not *garbage*. Masterpieces. I scooped my books into my arms and cradled them against my chest as I made my way to the living room without giving him a response. I was done with his negativity. He would never understand what these books meant to me because he couldn't wrap his mind around the lives they let me live.

I sat on the couch with a huff. "Do I say anything about the sports or video game books *you* read?"

"At least those things are real."

That was true. Each book I read immersed me in a world and relationship I would never experience. Whenever Michael rubbed my back while we watched the newest Netflix series, I would daydream about being taken on the kitchen counter or followed ruthlessly by a hot stranger. The stark contrast between our mundane relationship and the passion in those stories was hard to ignore.

"Games aren't real. I see no difference between you playing in a fake world and me reading one." *Checkmate.*

"Fair point," he said with a smile as he brushed his hand through his blond hair.

This was the marriage I needed to have. A healthy one. I once sought men who needed extensive therapy, requiring me to be their parent instead of their partner, which was a whole different problem. Michael was different. He was a kind, hardworking, and handsome partner. He only lacked things I selfishly desired for myself—he wasn't very affectionate, spontaneous, or open-minded—but his pros fully outweighed his cons. We were perfect for each other . . . outside the bedroom. In the bedroom, the differences between us equated to the distance between Mars and Jupiter. We were from different planets. If he'd only read one of those stories, he would have understood what made me tick, things I couldn't find the courage to mention myself.

I ragged on Michael for things I didn't give him a chance to change, but I wasn't the maestro of sex, either. I was too insecure about my thick thighs and the bit of chub beneath my shirt. I wasn't some model or porn star, and I felt that at my core when I had sex. Fuck me, but don't look at me, please. Every jiggle of my fat pulled me away from an orgasm. How could I come when I couldn't stop thinking about what to make for fucking dinner tomorrow or that I'd gone up a pants size again? I was sick of *thinking*. I wanted to be ravished so roughly that I couldn't think if I wanted to, but I loved Michael so much. If we synced up in the bedroom, we'd be perfect.

Michael finished putting the last of the groceries away and came toward the couch. He leaned over me, planting a kiss on the top of my head. It bugged me a bit because I wanted a real kiss. I wanted him to press his lips against mine with a hunger that said he needed me. But that wasn't *real*. We never fed a dangerous fire built from passion that risked burning everyone around us. We were just a smoldering glow.

"How was work?" he asked.

"Exhausting, as usual. I'm beginning to think I don't belong in customer service," I said with a sigh. "You?"

"Busy. The sweet embrace of death can come for me at any time." He flopped down beside me and grabbed his tablet from the coffee table.

"We are such positive people." I laughed. "Who wouldn't want to be around us?"

That's what our marriage looked like. Me with my nose in a book and Michael flicking away on his tablet. The raw and uncensored version of what it meant to be comfortable. I made it sound terrible, but I wouldn't have traded Michael for anyone, not even one of the men in my novels. Book boyfriends couldn't be your husband.

Michael kissed my lips before following a path down my chest. He was hard against his boxers, and I felt it through my cat pajama pants. So attractive, I know, but they were fucking comfortable. He fumbled with them until they slid off my legs—he'd never been the most graceful person—and his lips grazed my thighs. For a moment, I thought he would go down on me. Instead, he came up to kiss my lips once more.

When was the last time he ate me out? It had to have been on my birthday . . . two months ago. Why was I thinking about that? *Focus.*

He drew me back into the moment as he rubbed his warm cock against me. I didn't even realize he'd removed his boxers. Shit, that was terrible. His fingers rubbed between my legs, but I wasn't anywhere near wet enough for what he wanted to do. I looked over at the lube on the bedside table. It was just out of reach, and I was too tired to get out of bed to get it. I was too exhausted to care.

Somehow I managed to get wet enough from the half-hearted touch between my legs, and he pushed inside me with a groan. He fucked me but my mind wandered instead of focusing on the motions of his hips against me. I moaned softly. He still felt good, filling me just right, and he wasn't bad at sex. I was just bored. I couldn't blame him for that, and I wasn't exactly helping in the arousal department. I had stopped trying to look good for him, and I hated myself for it. Even though I disliked myself for doing that, I still didn't have the motivation to change it.

When had this become such a job for me? Something that felt like it had to be done to truly be husband and wife? When had I become such an old lady in a twenty-five-year-old body? I used to be wild and insatiable. I still was, but now those traits inhabited my brain, lurking through the shadowy places in my mind.

My thoughts wandered again, revisiting every book boyfriend I'd ever had. I closed my eyes and imagined their strong, fiery hands racing over me—a touch over-flowing with desire as harsh words left their lips. Every thrust made me feel like I didn't matter while also making me feel as if I was the *only* one who mattered.

Guilt filled my chest. *This is wrong. Fictional or not, it's wrong.*

I opened my eyes as Michael leaned down to bury his face in my neck. His thrusts slowed and pushed deeper inside me. He groaned and sent a warm breath rolling over my skin, leaving a longing inside me as he pulled away.

I cleaned myself off with a towel I kept by the bed and thought about the lack of clean-up in the books I read. No running to the bathroom. No tightening of muscles to keep come from dripping down their thighs. Just lying in the embrace of their lover, filled and happy.

I got up to pee. As my footfalls landed on the soft carpet on my way to the bathroom, my eyes roved over all the things that made this house a *home*. Our home. I worked, but he worked harder and for longer hours. He was the reason we had what we had, and I was being an ungrateful shit. But I couldn't stop myself from wanting more.

I firmly remind myself that my books weren't reality. My reality was boring, but that was what I needed. That was normal.

But sometimes I wanted more than normalcy, and that's where my books came into play. There was nothing average about any of these stories or the people within them. Their lives were full of angst and fast-paced drama. As hot as it was, that would be equally exhausting after a while. The men in the books weren't good for anyone. They were morally gray in all the sexy ways that made me melt, but they would have made my real life hell.

I washed my hands, returned to our room, and crawled into bed beside him. He'd already turned over and fallen asleep. I wished I could fall asleep like that.

I forgot to take care of that thing at work.

The meat in the fridge has a best-by date of . . . tomorrow.

Remember when my boss saw one of my books on my desk three years ago?

Oh, remember that kid in high school who tried to stealth me while we were having sex? Dude wasn't very fucking stealthy.

My thoughts drifted from the boy in high school to my first boyfriend, the boy who took my virginity. I became stuck in a haze of memories, recalling the excited hands of teenagers getting to do something they shouldn't do. The risk. It was all so electrifying.

My thoughts wandered even further down a rabbit hole of darkness. After replaying all the embarrassing moments from my past, I finally drifted into a well-earned sleep.

Chapter Two

T he sun shined its bright light through the curtains in my bedroom, reviving me from my restless sleep. Kinda. I opened my eyes with a groan. No matter how early I lay down, I tossed and turned for ages before I could finally fall asleep. I was always exhausted. Would I ever wake up feeling refreshed, or was this a permanent state of being for me at this point?

With another groan, I climbed out of bed. Michael had already left the bedroom, and his side of the bed was cool to the touch. He always got up before me. Early to bed and early to rise.

I sauntered into the kitchen and grabbed a cup of coffee from the pot Michael had brewed. I sniffed, inhaling the pleasant aroma. He always made everything perfect, yet I found myself feeling bitter instead of grateful. I sighed.

Still feeling exhausted, I headed into the living room and curled up on the couch with my favorite weighted blanket. Yes, I went straight from my bed to lying on the couch. I preferred the sedentary lifestyle, especially since I never had a moment to just exist on weekdays. Weekends were all for me.

Cuddled in the warmth of my own body heat, I looked at the tempting stack of books on the table. I wiggled my arm from under the blanket and grabbed the top book. The matte finish felt like velvet beneath my fingers. I touched the shadowy image of the shirtless, gray-haired man dominating the cover. He was the embodiment of a silver fox, and I was here for it. He was also the married, overbearing boss of the female main character, and who didn't love a forbidden man?

I sat up, rolled my sleeves up my arms, and wrapped the blanket around my lower body. I listened for Michael meandering about, but silence was the only reply. I opened the book, rested it on my lap, and let my eyes dance along the page as I absorbed every word. My mind was a blank canvas, ready for the art within each word.

The fictional world erupted from the floor and surrounded me. I lost touch with my reality and embraced the place where I could hide from my responsibilities. I had no accountability in that place, and I spent my time with people who made my heart race with anticipation and exhilaration.

My hand slipped into my sweatpants and found my growing excitement, making my fingers slick. I throbbed with expectation before the spine even made that satisfying crack when I first opened the book.

"Zoey?" The booming voice came from an office down the hall. I looked around at the empty cubicles. Everyone had already gone home, and the clock on my computer ticked past 7:30. I'd stayed too late—yet again—but I had nothing to go home to. Just a lonely apartment with a cat who hated me. I tapped a pencil on the desk as I tried to finish the last few minutes of the presentation I was listening to.

"Zoey!" The voice grew louder, and I pulled my earbud out of my ear with a sigh.

After locking my computer, I stood and smoothed my black skirt over my hips. The dingy blue carpet muffled the tap of my heels as I walked down the hall and stopped at the only other office still illuminated that late in the evening. I tucked my hair behind my ear, took a deep breath, and stepped into the doorway.

"Yes?" I asked.

The chair spun around to face me, and Mr. Lawrence's blue eyes looked me over. "I'm glad you're still here," he said in an even tone. He knew I stayed late almost every night. "Is there a reason the reports for the client haven't been submitted to me? I asked for them"— he moved his keyboard to look at the calendar on his desk —"last week."

Fuck. I knew I forgot something. It was a big thing too. Probably the single most important thing I was supposed to remember all year. "I . . . made a mistake." I had no excuse for why I forgot to get him the reports. Why he'd have to tell the bank tomorrow morning that he wasn't prepared. It didn't matter that it was my fault, because he would be the face of the failure. Yeah, I fucked up. "I forgot."

He stared at me, his lips taut. "You forgot? You aren't going to lie and make it seem like you aren't this incompetent?" His normally handsome features twisted in anger, which I deserved. I *was* incompetent, and I deserved to be fired for such a colossal fuck up, but I silently pleaded for mercy. I needed this job.

"I'm sorry," I said, dropping my gaze. I had nothing more to say.

Mr. Lawrence's chair squeaked as he pushed it away from his desk. The wheels snagged on the shitty carpet. He stood, walked toward me, and took a seat on the corner of the desk. The intense way he stared at me made me swallow hard. I felt like I had a golf ball in my throat.

He brushed a hand through his salt-and-pepper hair. "You're a good employee, Zoey. Smart, witty, well-versed, really quite the asset here."

"But?" *Please don't fire me, please don't fire me.*

"This is a massive fuck up. What am I supposed to say at the meeting tomorrow? I can't tell them that my employee simply *forgot* the most important thing I had to bring besides myself."

"Am I fired?" I asked. I was torn because I hated my job, but my livelihood depended on it.

Mr. Lawrence walked to the coat rack in the corner of his office and shrugged out of his suit jacket before hanging it up. He loosened the neck of his blue tie, which sat tucked beneath his crisp checkered dress shirt. "No. I'm not firing you. I'll just make a night out of it and do the reports myself." He sounded disappointed, and his soft tone confused me. He should have been mad. "You're twenty-something, right, Zoey?"

I cleared my throat. "Twenty-five."

"I have thirty years on you, and I don't forget important parts of my job like you do. Shouldn't this be the other way around?" He smirked as he walked back to the corner of his desk and sat on the dark, expensive wood.

It was hard to get reprimanded by him without thinking of him bending me over the desk and letting me know what a shitty employee I'd been. I imagined him raising my skirt and using his big, firm hand to punish me exactly how I deserved. This fuck up would get me so many spankings I wouldn't be able to sit down for a week. Heat flushed my cheeks at the thought, and I hoped he didn't notice.

"D-Do you need anything else?" I asked, getting hung up on my words.

Mr. Lawrence rolled up his sleeves. "How long have you worked here, Zoey?"

"Almost five years."

"And in those five years, have I ever made you uncomfortable?"

"What? No." I laughed nervously, swiping my sweaty palms on my skirt.

"Then why are you acting so nervous?" he asked with a genuine smile as he reached out and casually turned over the picture of his wife.

"Well, like you said, I made a colossal mistake."

Mr. Lawrence grabbed a ball from his desk and tossed it between his hands. His big, strong hands. He noticed me staring. "Oh, Zoey, I don't know how to broach this topic with you."

"I can stay and do the reports," I blurted.

"That's not what I mean."

He stepped toward me and touched the collar of my dress shirt. I held my breath as he pulled his hand away. My eyes trailed down the checkered pattern of his pressed shirt, stopping at his broad chest. I let my gaze fall until it reached his expensive slacks. Even through the pleated pattern of his pants, I could see how hard he was. It was undeniable.

I bit my lip. "What do you mean?" I thought I knew what he meant, but I couldn't believe it was happening. Was it *really* happening?

"I have wanted you for a few years now. It's unbearable." His blue eyes softened further, and there was a throb in his angular jaw, as if he wasn't sure if this was worth the risk.

It was. I was certain of that.

Did he know how much I fantasized about him? Why I often dropped my gaze when he looked at me? How I couldn't focus on his reprimands because my mind wandered to his cock? I wanted to know what waited beneath his suit. Even the way he said my name made me question if he was as demanding in the bedroom as he was in the workplace. I had made myself come to the answers to those questions more often than I cared to admit.

"Isn't this against policy?" I choked out. I would break the shit out of that policy tonight. The rules didn't matter to me, but I expected my question to bring him to his senses, and I waited for the realization to wash the hunger from his face.

"Very much so. I would lose my job. But I can't stop thinking about your pussy." He tossed the ball back to the desk.

His words made my jaw drop.

"I hope I'm not being too forward, Zoey," he said in the most seductive yet fatherly tone.

"No . . . no . . . you aren't."

Mr. Lawrence's warm breath brushed along the skin of my chest, making goosebumps scatter and rise to the surface. He leaned in and kissed me. His clean-shaven face was smooth against mine, and he smelled like aftershave. His hand drifted around the back of my neck and grabbed the clip securing my hair, pulling it from its place. My auburn locks tumbled down, falling over my shoulders.

"I want you to make it up to me." He brushed his fingers through my hair, fisting it at the nape of my neck.

"Make what up to you?" I asked. I knew what I needed to make up to him, but I wanted to hear more of his sultry and commanding words.

He smirked. "All this time I'll have to spend finishing the work *you* didn't bother to do." His words were harsh, and they made me clench my legs. I crossed them to try to calm the throbbing.

"How can I do that?" I asked with feigned naivety, but I knew what he wanted. I saw it through his pants. He was so damn hard, tenting his slacks.

Mr. Lawrence unbuckled his belt, and the clang of metal made me shiver. I kept my eyes locked on his large hands as he unbuttoned his slacks, focusing on the veins. The sound of his falling zipper broke the sticky silence of the office, and I worried the room would combust from all the erotic tension. His pants splayed open, exposing his cock. His length was impressive, even more so than I fantasized about, and I bit my lip as I watched him grab himself and stroke. I wanted to be the hand caressing the soft skin of his dick.

"On your knees," he commanded in the exact tone of a man with that much authority over me.

He didn't need to tell me twice. I dropped to my knees, the carpet rubbing my bare skin. He grabbed my hand and placed it on him. I stroked him, moving along his swollen and excited head. He fisted my hair again and pushed his cock into my mouth. The scent of his masculine cologne overpowered me, and I breathed it in and absorbed it into my memory.

His head dropped back as if I had been the touch he'd been waiting for, like my mouth was what he needed. He grabbed the back of my head and forced himself deeper into my mouth, fucking my face, smearing my red lipstick on my porcelain skin, staining my cheek.

He pulled his dick out of my mouth and rubbed his thumb along my lower lip. "Do you think that's enough for the hours of work I'll have to do tonight? Just that perfect mouth of yours?"

I shook my head as I got to my feet and wiped at my mouth with the back of my hand. It wasn't enough.

He raked his arm across his desk, sending his cupholder flying and pens and pencils skittering across the carpet. The hurried and sloppy way he needed me didn't keep him from finding my mouth as he laid me down. I pulled his keyboard from beneath my lower back and shoved it aside. My hip knocked over the framed photo of his family. His hands raced up my thighs as he bunched my skirt at my hips and rubbed his fingers against my soaked panties. The touch made me tremble. I wanted this as much as he did.

He pulled my panties aside, exposing my pussy, and I felt insecurity rise into my clenching stomach as someone as perfect as him looked down at something he'd wanted for so long. What if I wasn't what he expected? I didn't want him to regret taking such a risk on me. What if I was *everything* he expected? What would that mean for us? I'd be tempted to *forget* more work so I could get this punishment. He groaned as he rubbed his fingers over my swollen, excited clit. His touch made me shudder, too sensitive for his rough hands.

Mr. Lawrence shoved two fingers inside me, then three. I gasped, having always admired those large, strong hands, and now I felt every curve of them as they thrust inside me. Plunging his fingers deeper, he leaned over and kissed me again. My thighs trembled as he stood and palmed his dripping cock. He rubbed it against me, warm and wet with arousal, and my excitement coated him as he surged into me with ease. His fingers sank into my hips as he gripped them and fucked me. His desk shook, causing more things to fall to the floor. I worried his monitor would slip from the edge as it tilted closer, but his harder thrusts told me it didn't matter if it did.

"Unbutton your shirt," he commanded.

I did as I was told, unfastening every button until my

shirt splayed open and exposed my breasts beneath a black bra. His fingers grazed my cleavage before he grabbed the straps and pulled them down, pushing the fabric away and freeing my chest. He dropped his lips to my nipples, swirling his tongue around them and sucking until I moaned.

"I want to see you bent over my desk," he said.

Mr. Lawrence grabbed my hips and pulled me off the desk. He turned me around and leaned me over the wood. His hands raced to lift my skirt again, bunching it at my waist. He groped my ass with a rough grasp that pulled a whimper from my throat. It was exactly how I fantasized. Instead of stopping to ask if I was okay with it, he pushed me against the desk until my breasts pressed against the wood.

He leaned over me, his breath warming my ear. "I can't believe how much work you've left me," he said with a snarl as he smacked my ass, etching a deep sting within my skin. He drew his hand back and struck me again.

I bit my lip against the pain, trying to keep from screaming out. My skin still flamed with warmth, even as his hand left me with an imprint that remained long after he wound up for another slap. He struck me harder, gripping my ass at the end of the swing. I whimpered, unable to ignore the discomfort as his repeated hits bit at me. He wasn't holding back. Not even a little. I deserved that pain because I was a real shitty employee.

"Zoey," he groaned. "You disappointed me. Caused me so much more work. Work that I shouldn't need to do because I have people like *you* to do it for me." He drew his hand back and smacked me once more, pressing me harder against the desk. "You were a bad employee, Zoey, but you're being *such* a good girl," he growled as he used his knee to spread my legs.

The way he said my name and called me a good girl made me tremble in anticipation. As he pushed inside me again, I gasped and grabbed the edge of the desk to steady myself. He fucked me so hard I forgot he was fifty-five. I forgot he was my boss. I forgot my own goddamn name.

"You feel exactly how I imagined you'd feel," he said.

"How do I feel?" I asked with heavy breaths. I wanted to hear him tell me.

"Tight. Perfect. Like you need to be filled."

"Don't come in me," I whispered, my body tensing at the mention of it.

He lifted me by my hair and kissed the nape of my neck. "I will come wherever I want," he growled into my ear.

I couldn't say no to him.

He was my boss.

He pushed me down and grabbed my skirt, using it as a strap as he pounded me harder. With a gravelly moan, his hips slowed their assault on my ass as he came inside me. I felt him pulse deep within me as he filled me.

"Zoey," he said. Pleasure laced my name. He lifted me by my hair. "I was forgiving this time, but don't fuck me over again, sweet girl, or next time, I'll take your ass too."

I came. Hard. My thighs trembled as I pulled my fingers from my panties. Footfalls came from down the hall, and I tried to quiet my heavy breaths. I slammed the book closed and pulled the blanket over me, wiping my come onto my pants.

"Morning," Michael said as he sat beside me with a cup of coffee. He grabbed my leg beneath the blanket and rubbed it.

I had guilt in my gut from my orgasm. I had imagined being fucked by someone else while my husband was in the next room. I loved Michael, but he would never fuck me with a burning desire like that.

No, a *need*. I wanted him to *need* me.

Michael cooked us breakfast as usual on weekend mornings, and we sat together and ate in silence. There was no need for forced conversation or charades. We were comfortable. I stared at him as he pushed eggs around his plate with his fork. With his glasses perched on his slender nose, he glanced up at me with the ice-blue eyes I fell in love with.

"Why are you staring at me? Creep," he asked with a chuckle. He wiped his face with a paper towel and used his other hand to smooth down the hairs of his well-groomed beard.

There was so much to love about him. About us. Yet there I was, longing to push those plates off the kitchen table and have him take me right there, right then. He was oblivious to the fire in my eyes as the longing for his cock engulfed me. I stood, pushed what was left on my plate into the trash, and placed it in the sink. I kissed him, wrapping my arms around his shoulders.

"I'm going to go shower, if you want to join."

"To be boiled alive? No thanks," he said with a laugh. Yet another thing we didn't have in common. He liked tepid showers. I liked to leave the shower with reddened skin. The heat of the burning-hot water soothed me.

I hadn't purchased the multi-feature showerhead for nothing. I'd come with the heat surrounding and embracing me. I'd envision Michael fucking me for being the incompetent wife I felt I was.

Chapter Three

M ichael was working late again. Nights like that, when the sun set and the sky darkened and he still wasn't home, I knew sex would be the last thing on his mind. A well-deserved beer and kicking his feet up would be his first priority, as it should be.

I grabbed a new book off the table as I headed to my bedroom. Excitement rose with each padded footstep. My body knew what was coming. The aching desire to disappear into a new world with no job, meals to cook, or a house to clean . . . it was like an addiction. And I needed my fix.

I slipped beneath the white down comforter on the bed I'd made that morning. It was cold at first and would remain that way until my body heat warmed it up, and I planned on turning that heat way up. I propped up the pillows and scooted back against them. The book lay on the bed beside me, and the cover drew me in immediately. A mouth-watering bearded man stood beside a motorcycle and looked menacingly back at me as if he were looking through me. Tattoos covered his body, and a scar ran down his cheek. He looked angry, but once my eyes found his bulging muscles beneath his t-shirt, I didn't care. It'd been a while since I'd read a dark motor-cycle-gang story, and I was more than ready to slip into this world. I prepared myself for the grungy, rough-and-tumble attitude of a gang of bikers. It wouldn't involve sweet lovemaking, and I was more than okay with that.

The story sucked me into an unfamiliar yet tanta-lizing environment where everything had different mean-ings and the people had a customary way of doing and saying things. I could envision the club's president, his leather cut resting over a black t-shirt. Harsh. Intolerable. Rough. I could imagine his son, who the author described as selfish but kind. She detailed these men in an artistic way, and I wanted all of it. The more I read, the more wet I became. It was just dirty enough, with a touch of violence. Beautiful violence.

I looked at the clock on my phone, making sure Michael wouldn't be home for a while longer. I slipped off my leggings and tossed them on the floor beside the bed. I rubbed myself through my panties, letting the soft material create friction against my touch as the harsh MC world engulfed me.

Loud music blared through the large modern clubhouse, and a wraparound bar greeted us the moment the club president and I walked in. Several men in cuts turned to look at me before greeting the president with nods of recognition and respect. High-top tables were scattered throughout, their worn wooden surfaces resting atop rusty posts attached to dirty bases. Girls in short skirts bent over the pool table and pretended to play while men stood around chugging beers and tugging on their leather jackets. One of the men slid his hand up a girl's skirt and played with her as if they weren't surrounded by a crowd of people. A motorcycle stood on a platform on the other side of the room, and framed photos of bikes and their owners lined the walls. In the pictures, the members were standing beside their bikes or straddling the seats, sometimes with a woman, but usually alone.

The bartender slid a beer over the bar top and into the grasp of the man beside me—the club president. Amber liquid sloshed over the sides of the glass, and he rubbed his graying blond beard before chugging his drink. I looked up at him. He had nearly two feet of height on me, and he was as muscled as he was tall. An aged scar decorated his cheek, adding to his allure and conjuring images of a vicious brawl where he alone emerged victorious.

"Who's this?" the bartender asked with a throaty voice, as if she was born smoking a cigarette.

"A bike whore," he said. He looked down at me with menacing brown eyes and a wicked grin.

The words should have hurt my feelings, but that was precisely what I wanted to be, even if I wasn't entirely sure I could handle it. I flashed him an unsure smile. It was too late to get cold feet now. I rubbed my hand down my leather skirt to soothe my nerves.

The woman cleared her throat and nodded as she

passed a cold bottle of beer to me. I didn't open it. I wanted to be sure I remembered every dirty detail of whatever happened next. As the icy glass chilled my fingers, the president guided me down a wide set of wooden stairs and brought me into a finished basement. I looked around with wide eyes as the small group of men froze at the sight of me. One stopped mid-stroke with his pool stick. Another paused with a drink just below his lips. The president sat on an overstuffed couch in front of a huge TV that nearly took up half the wall. He pulled me onto his lap, and I rushed to pull my skirt down as I fell into him.

"J, who you got there?" asked a man leaning against a red wall covered in patches.

"This? She's a bike whore. Couldn't wait to hop on," J said in a gritty voice. "What's your name again, angel?"

"Zoey," I said without a fiber of confidence inside me.

"Can't hear you," called the man against the wall.

"Zoey," I said louder.

J's hand rubbed down my back and grabbed my ass in a bruising grip. My cheeks flushed. I loved bikers but that was the first time I'd ever been to a clubhouse. I'd fucked a biker before, but never on his turf. I swam in the warm pool of excitement, ready to get yanked below the surface.

J rubbed his beard, brushing the scraggly hairs down. I watched his arms as they wrapped around my waist. Faded tattoos covered them, but one caught my eye—a red heart with the name Roxy scrawled inside.

"Is that your old lady?" I asked as I pointed to the name. The men roared with laughter.

'That's his bike," said the younger man playing pool. He dropped the pool stick onto the table and walked toward us. He pulled a bandana from his neck onto his head pushing his long, dark hair out of his face. "Ain't it, J? He never loved my mother the way he loved that bike."

"Fuck off, son." J flipped him off, then nodded to me. "This is Sonny."

Clever.

Sonny flopped onto the couch, leaned back, and rested his head on his hands. My eyes roved over him, scrutinizing him. A short, dark beard blanketed his jaw, and eyes as black as leather looked back at me. His tight white t-shirt rode up his abdomen, exposing his fit stomach and the happy trail wandering below the waistband of his jeans.

"Where'd you get her from?" Sonny asked with a raised eyebrow.

"Don't matter where I got her from." He released a low moan as he rubbed his large hand up my thigh. "All that matters is that she's here for us to use."

"No shit?" Sonny said with a smile. "All of us?"

I bit my lip and nodded. I wanted each one of them inside me.

"She doesn't look like she can handle much." J brushed back my hair and gripped my neck. "But I'll make sure she takes what she can."

"Bear!" Sonny called out, peering around the clubhouse basement.

"Yeah?" asked a deep voice from around a corner. As he entered the room, I expected a big man like J, but Bear was a short, muscular bald man.

"She's going to let us all have a turn with her," Sonny said with a smirk.

Bear rubbed his hands together. "Is that so?"

"Why do they call you Bear?" I asked.

Bear laughed. "Because I can't grow hair for shit. My face is as smooth as a woman's ass." It was true.

Sonny and Bear both had such young faces. Even with the beard covering Sonny's chin, they both looked much sweeter and less hardened than J. But looks could be deceiving, and I knew they wouldn't be sweet or gentle lovers.

Bear turned back toward the room he'd come from and shouted for someone else. "Shotgun!"

Another man came from the other room, twisting his mustache between his fingers as he walked closer. He was slightly older and wore a bandana around his neck. "What's up?"

"We're going to have quite the time tonight, brother." Sonny gestured toward me. Heat painted my cheeks.

Shotgun brushed his hand through his short blond hair.

"Why do they call you shotgun? Is it because you're afraid of guns?" I asked with a playful smile.

Shotgun was much more serious as he shook his head and retrieved his shotgun from the other room. I tensed at the sight of it. He pulled shells from the side saddle and loaded the gun.

"It's a Holland & Holland custom with an engraved receiver." He stroked it with a loving hand. "My baby." His muscular arms flexed as he handled his weapon and erotically rubbed the cool metal with a big, strong hand.

Shotgun, much like J, was grungy and big bodied, intimidating as the cords of his muscles flexed with something he wanted within his grasp. Me and that gun.

"When are we doing this?" Sonny asked, rubbing his hand up my other thigh.

"Not till I'm done with her," J quipped. He gripped my ass before pushing me off his lap and dropping me onto the couch. With a big stretch and a cocky grin, he stood and reached for the chain attached to his belt loop. His jeans splayed open as he unfastened the belt, and he tugged his boxers down, placing his cock in front of my face. "Come on, angel, you know what I want you to do." He reached out and grabbed my chin, running a rough thumb across my lips.

"Right here? In front of everyone?" My jaw went slack.

"What did you think? We all want to see or feel that pretty mouth of yours."

"Don't forget that sweet pussy," Sonny said with a focused stare as he leaned over and reached up my skirt.

"Get up," J said, more commanding that time.

I stood and he took my spot on the couch, leaning back and stroking his cock as his eyes trailed over me. I dropped to my knees on the cold tile floor, and he shook his cock in my face. Sensing my hesitation, he fisted my hair and pushed me down until I took him into my mouth. He smelled of body wash and a musk that wasn't unpleasant. I took his full length in my mouth, running my tongue up and down as my hand gripped the base of his cock and stroked. He let out a gruff groan as I sucked him off.

Someone lifted my skirt until the leather got stuck on the cuffs of my ass. I tried to pull away to look back, but J held my head in his lap, gripping my hair and forcing me down. Rough hands grabbed at my ass and smacked it, but I couldn't tell who it was.

"You are soaked," said the voice behind me. He grabbed the waistband of my panties and pulled them down, leaving them at my thighs. Fingers prodded at me, spreading me. "Bear, look at this *pussy*."

It's Sonny. I could tell by the way he said the word. He rubbed me before pushing his fingers inside. I heard the rattle of his belt buckle as it came undone, and my heart raced. Was this really happening?

Sonny put his hands on my waist, wiping my wetness back onto me. He squeezed my hips and surged inside me, thrusting me against his father's lap. His hips smacked against me. His hands roved over my ass and slapped it so hard that I had to pull J's cock out of my mouth to keep from accidentally biting him.

J grabbed my chin and lifted it until I looked him in the eye. "You like when Sonny fucks you, angel?" He groaned as he looked over at his son, still pounding into me. "My old lady would kill me if I fucked you," he said with a devilish smile, "but it won't stop me from coming down your throat."

He pushed my head down and thrust his hips upward, forcing himself deeper into my mouth. I stifled a gag and pulled away to moan as Sonny sped up his thrusts. J shoved himself back into my mouth. With heavy breaths pouring from my nose, I tried not to moan as Sonny pounded his hips against me.

J used my hair to guide my head, and he quickened his motions as his hips met my mouth. With a groan and a final deep thrust of his hips, he came without warning. I gagged from the unexpected warmth hitting the back of my throat and pulled away, wiping my mouth.

J stroked my hair. "Thanks, angel," he said as he got up, leaving me gripping the now vacant couch cushion as his son continued to fuck me from behind.

Sonny ran a hand up my shirt and squeezed the flesh of my chest as he pulled me against him. "Why are you still wearing a fucking shirt?" He growled against my ear and supported my upper body as I pulled my shirt over my head and tossed it aside. His fingers rubbed along the bare skin of my back. "I wanna be the last one inside her," he said as he pulled out and sat in front of me. "Taste yourself."

He grabbed himself and held it in front of my lips. He was much bigger than J, and slick with my wetness. With long, drawn-out motions, he stroked himself in front of my lips. It made my mouth water, and I stifled the desire with his dick, tasting my sweetness.

He groaned and dropped his head back. "I don't know what feels better, your mouth or your cunt."

"Who's taking her for a ride next?" came a voice from somewhere beside me.

"She's all yours, Bear," Sonny said with a groan. He pulled me away by my hair and touched my lips with his fingers. "Well, this is mine."

Bear unfastened his belt, and the metallic clang sent a shiver of excitement through me. His hands raced over me before smacking my ass and gripping it after the final slap. A moan escaped my lips as Bear thrust into me from behind. He grunted and fucked me with slow and rhythmic movements, as if making sure he could feel every inch of me. His thick cock made me moan again, but Sonny shoved himself into my mouth, effectively silencing me. Bear continued pumping inside me until I felt a tightening in my gut. Heat enveloped my body, and my thighs quivered. It was ecstasy to have Bear behind me and Sonny in my mouth.

I pulled Sonny away from my lips with a groan. I had to. With my hand wrapped around his cock, I dropped my head between his legs and stroked him with wet fingers.

"Keep at it, Bear. You're gonna make her come," Sonny said through a growl. "Come for me," Sonny commanded, gripping my hair in his fist. "Come so I can take that sweet mouth again."

His words made me tremble and pushed me over the edge. I came hard and bit my lip to stifle the screams that teased my tongue. I sat back against Bear, pushing him deeper as I spasmed.

"Fuck," I whimpered.

"You like that?" Sonny asked as he fisted my hair. I nodded my head and looked up with pleading eyes. Noticing Bear's quickening thrusts, he furrowed his brow. "Don't you come in her, Bear."

"But . . ." Bear groaned and I flashed my eyes back at him.

"Come on her ass, on her face, down her throat, I don't care. Just not inside her pussy." Sonny's voice was firm with a hint of irritation. I looked up at him, longing to feel him inside me again, however he wanted it.

Bear pulled out and stroked himself against my ass. He finished and used my shirt to clean the warm come from my skin.

"Shotgun, make it fast. I can't wait much longer for her," Sonny said with a devilish smile that rivaled his father's as he zipped up his jeans and sat on the far end of the long couch. He picked up the beer bottle I left on the floor, popped it open, and took a drink.

Shotgun came up beside me, blocking my view of Sonny. He twirled his mustache before grabbing me by the arm and lifting me to my feet. He lay back on the couch with one leg bent and still firm on the floor, unzipped his jeans, and pulled out his cock. I stepped out of my panties and let them fall to the ground. He grabbed me and pulled me onto his lap, and I whimpered as I lowered myself onto him. His length pushed into me until it hurt, and his deep thrusts made my gut ache. His hands groped my chest, and he tugged at my nipples. He moved his hips and forced his dick even further.

"You are a fine piece of ass, aren't you?" Shotgun groaned as he held my hips and sped up my movements, thrusting harder to meet me in the middle. His hands reached around and grabbed my ass, squeezing it as he pushed his hips into me.

I felt a hand on the small of my back, and it pushed me forward until my breasts pressed against Shotgun's chest. I gasped, wrapped my arms around his neck, and rode him, grinding my hips and rocking against him.

"God," Sonny growled behind me. "Seeing you ass

up like that makes me want to use you." He got up, and his steps toward me made me shiver.

The cool froth of beer landed on my ass as he poured the last bit of his drink on me. He rubbed his finger against me before pushing it inside. I gasped, tightening around Shotgun's cock and making him groan. Sonny spit behind me and before I could tell him no, he pushed the neck of the bottle into my ass. My body tensed at the intrusive feeling of the cold, smooth glass, and I bit back the moment of discomfort as I stretched around it. He groaned and worked the bottle in and out of me as Shotgun continued to thrust beneath me. I felt full, but I wished it was Sonny's cock instead of a bottle.

Sonny spit again and began to rub his cock with slow and sensual strokes, and the way his hand wrapped around himself made me hungry for him. "You'll take anything we can give you, huh?" he asked as he pushed the neck of the bottle inside me with his crotch. He fisted my hair as if he were fucking me with his cock instead of glass. The smell of beer wafted up to me.

"You could use your cock," I whispered. I'd rather feel the familiarity of that than the bottle.

He smirked. "Oh no, I'm saving that because I'm going to fuck your tight cunt again. You'll wait for it like a good whore." His words made me twitch between my legs.

"I wanna come on your pretty face," Shotgun moaned.

Sonny pulled the bottle out of me and set it on the table. He helped me to my feet, tugging me off Shotgun's lap and pushing me to my knees by my shoulders. He drew the hair from my face and craned my neck, forcing me to look up at Shotgun as he stood. Shotgun held the base of himself to keep from coming before my mouth opened for him. My lips parted with eager anticipation, and he painted my tongue with his come, finishing with a final flick onto my cheeks. I licked my lips, tasting the salty remnants of pleasure as I looked up at Sonny.

"Wipe that shit off your face," he said with a rough voice as he released his grasp on my hair. I grabbed my shirt from the floor and cleaned my face as he commanded. He lifted me to my feet and grabbed my arm, dragging me toward the pool table. He picked me up and set me on the rail, and I held myself up with my hands as I leaned back and spread my legs. "That's what I've been waiting for," he said as he tugged me closer to the edge and let his warm cock rest against my pussy.

Sonny wrapped a hand around the back of my neck, dragged himself against me as he drew his hips back, and pushed himself inside me once more. He leaned over me, his breath hot in my face as he gripped the back of my head and started slamming into me. The pool table creaked with every thrust.

"Open wider for me," he growled.

I was open as wide as I could get for him, but he spread my legs further and moved his hand to the front of my neck with a rough grip. His other hand slid behind me and squeezed my ass, pulling me against him. I felt his touch everywhere. It was too much, bringing me close to the edge all over again. My pussy was stretched and used and so sore, yet I still wanted more of Sonny.

"I'm going to fill you up," his groan was gravelly and

thick as he pulled my hips against his, giving me no choice but to take his come. His thrusts slowed and he kissed me, releasing a satiated moan against my mouth. "Such a perfect whore," he whispered as he pulled away from the kiss, his cock still throbbing inside me.

My fingers slowed, my heartbeat calmed, and I dropped the book in my lap. I came so many times I lost count. I rubbed my hands over my breasts, enjoying the feel of my sensitive flesh. The front door slammed, making me jump, and the book fell to the floor with an ominous thud. I rushed out of bed, snatched my pants from the floor, and pulled them on. The door cracked open. Michael stood there with his tie undone and bags under his eyes. He looked tired.

"What are you doing in here?" he asked, lifting his eyebrow as his head swiveled around to check the room.

"Just getting dressed. I'll be right out."

"Okay." He looked at me like I was having an affair. I would never.

Not in real life, at least.

Chapter Four

"This has been the longest week ever," I said with a groan as I sat at the table. I lived for the weekends. To do absolutely nothing and *not* be around people. "Are you sure you have to work tomorrow?" I asked with a pout of my lips. I knew the answer.

He slid a heaping plate of ziti in front of me and cocked his head. "You know I do. You act like I *want* to be away from you on the weekends."

"I know. I know." I looked at the clock behind him on the stove as I lifted my fork and stabbed at the sauce-covered pasta. I normally loved ziti, but my stomach was tense and I had no appetite for the meal he'd slaved over. I forced down as much as I could. "I'm going to go read in the bedroom for a little while, I think. Maybe it will ease my headache."

"That seems like it would do the opposite," he said with furrowed brows.

What I planned to do would definitely help with the headache. I brushed what was left of my uneaten food into the garbage and put my plate in the sink. Heading toward the back of the house, I passed the framed pictures decorating the hallway. Our wedding photo greeted me the moment I walked into the bedroom. It never failed to make me smile because of the expressions of pure contentment on our faces.

I grabbed a book off the table, lay in the bed, and pulled the soft, warm comforter over me. I curled up on my side and let my head hit the pillow as I studied the book's cover. It featured a man bathed in shadows. The light only illuminated his tough, handsome face beneath the hood of his open jacket. Tattoos crossed his bare chest. He looked menacing, but not in the same way the biker had. This image captured the essence of one-sided infatuation. Frustration. Jealousy. Possessiveness.

I opened the book and started reading. The crisp new pages turned faster than any of the others I'd read so far. Consent didn't matter in this world. It hardly existed.

I rested my hand beneath the waistband of my pants, ready for what was to come.

I got out of my car and walked the half block toward my house. No one peppered the sidewalks this late in the evening, not like the morning rush when children and parents preparing for school and people heading to their day jobs waited everywhere I turned. I hated walking in the dark, but I'd stayed too late at the office—yet again— which meant there were no parking spots on the road. Snow fell in thick flakes, sticking to everything around me. I shivered and stepped over the pile of snow covering the sidewalk as the night air blanketed me. My unfortunate heel found the hidden patch of ice on the other side, and I flailed my arms with a yelp. Just as I had accepted my fate and started to fall, strong arms wrapped around me.

"Whoa there. It's icy," the man said with a sweet smile. Flakes of snow landed in his dark hair, and haunted lines surrounded his rich amber eyes.

I blinked up at him, thankful he'd caught me but uneasy because I hadn't noticed him before now. "I guess it is," I said with a flush of heat rising into my cheeks despite the bitter temperature.

He steadied me, his grasp clinging to my hips a moment too long. His rough hand hovered over mine. "Don't you live in the blue house? The one with the big—"

"The magnolia tree. That's the only way people know my house. Forget all the money I spent on the rest of the landscaping."

"Yeah, the magnolia tree. You best be getting yourself inside." With a wave of his hand, he gestured toward my home. "I'm glad I finally got to meet you, neighbor." He smiled again, put his hood up, and walked the other way until the thick snowfall obscured him from view.

When I reached my house, my fingers were too numb to open the door at first. I fumbled with the ring of keys until I finally unlocked it and slipped inside, shivering as the heat embraced me. The snow began to melt on my jacket as I shrugged it off, and I brushed my hand through my hair before hanging up my scarf. The walls creaked from the cold. Evenings in the winter always seemed to be darker and gloomier, as if heavy with desolation, but it was always extra eerie on those late nights.

After making my way to the kitchen, I thumbed through old takeout and leftovers. I settled for Thai from . . . probably not that long ago. I smelled it as I opened the container before placing it into the microwave. Hints of cinnamon, peppers, and cumin tried to mask the slightly off undertones of old food, but that didn't deter me. Heating it up would nuke any bacteria. The sound of the microwave's closing door echoed through the silence filling the house.

As I started the microwave, a familiar odor wafted over me. Not Thai food, but a sweet, musky scent with a bit of a floral note weaving through it. I followed it until I reached my bedroom, where the smell was strongest.

"Why do I keep smelling that?" I asked myself. It wasn't the first time the mystery scent had grabbed my attention in my house.

The microwave beeped and the smell of reheated food overpowered the odd perfume I'd been chasing. I returned to the kitchen, pulled the questionable takeout from the microwave, and tasted it. An acrid snap of flavor at the end of the bite told me it was definitely off. I curled my lip and tossed the rest into the garbage.

"Fuck it," I groaned. I'd just have to eat tomorrow.

I went back to the bedroom to change out of my work clothes, but my zipper got stuck as I tried to unzip my dress. I contorted my body in ways I never knew I could, but I couldn't reach the damn thing. I tried to lift the dress over my head and got it to my hips before it snagged. "Damn baby-bearing hips," I muttered. Well, now what? Cut the damn thing? I grabbed a pair of vanity scissors off the dresser and brought it up to the strap of the dress.

"Don't cut it," said a voice behind me. "That's my favorite dress you wear."

I jumped, frozen with fear as I recognized that voice. It was the man from outside.

My heart thumped against my chest as his footsteps drew closer. Before I knew what was happening, his hot breath landed on my shoulder and melted the ice in my veins. I looked at the open bedroom door and bolted for it. My heartbeat urged me on with its galloping beat, and my fingers stretched in front of me, desperate to reach the knob. As my skin met with the metal, he grabbed me around the waist and effortlessly pulled me backward in a tight grip. I screamed and tried to hit him, flailing my hands and throwing my body backward against his broad chest.

"Stop, Zoey, I'm trying to help you," he said through clenched teeth. How did he know my name?

"Please let me go," I pleaded.

"I will if you don't run." I got a whiff of his cologne. A floral, musky scent that had been drifting in and out of my house for a while.

The fuck? "Who the hell are you?" I screamed as he put me down and slowly released his hold in case I tried to run again.

"I'm Anthony."

"Why the hell are you in my house? Have you

been . . . stalking me?" I grabbed the scissors and took a step back.

"Not stalking you, but I've been watching you," he said with a shrug, like that was completely normal fucking behavior.

"Since when?"

"We met at a bar. Well, we didn't really *meet*, but I saw you at a bar. You're so beautiful, Zoey." His bright eyes softened and his jaw relaxed. "Just perfection."

"You need to leave!" I raised the hand gripping the scissors, preparing myself to thrust them into him if he came a step closer.

"Or what?" He rushed forward, grabbed my wrist, and wrenched the scissors from me before tossing them across the room. "That's better," he said as he pressed his body into me. His hand wrapped around my waist and gripped the zipper on the back of my dress. He eased it down, allowing the fabric to spread and expose my back. His hand grazed my spine, sending goosebumps rising along my skin.

"Fuck you," I hissed. I balled my free hand into a fist.

"Oh no, it is not I who will be getting fucked." His smile twisted into a sadistic grin. He turned me around and shoved me against the dresser, knocking the wind out of me as the aged wood creaked beneath my weight. "Don't think I didn't see your fist. If you hit me, I can't guarantee both of us will leave this house alive, but if you're a good girl, I'll let you choose if you're breathing or not when I fuck you." He kept his voice even as he spoke, and he ran his hand down my back once more. "Your skin is so soft." He panted against the nape of my neck. His words made me shiver and his touch made my goose-bumps spread.

"What the hell is wrong with you?" I screamed as he pressed his weight into me, pinning me against the dresser.

"There is absolutely nothing wrong with me. I'm in love. There's nothing wrong with that," he said with a groan as he grabbed the straps of my dress and pulled them off my shoulders. He sniffed my skin with a sultry moan, like he'd been imagining doing just that for too long. "Be a good girl and take the dress off your arms."

I hesitated and he leaned into me more. I pulled the straps off and the top of my dress fell. His cock hardened and pressed against my ass.

"Please . . ."

He reached over and pulled my hair across my back and over my shoulder. He grabbed my chin roughly, letting his hand drop to my throat. "No sense in begging. I'm going to take what I've wanted for months."

I had to think of something. I had to stop him from assaulting me. Maybe if I played his game, he'd back up enough to give me a chance to escape.

"I know," I whispered with a subtle bite of my lip. "I want it too." While I thought I was only telling him what he wanted to hear, I couldn't deny the confused tingle of pressure between my legs. His rough, demanding touch almost excited me.

Anthony laughed humorlessly. "Nice try."

His scent wrapped me in an embrace, and I breathed it in. He smelled like a friend, like someone I had curled up with in bed. I tried to remember how long that smell had been a part of my home. How many times he'd been in the same house, the same room as me. The thought oddly exhilarated me, and the fear only fueled the heat between my legs.

His hand climbed my thighs and pulled my panties aside. He rubbed his fingers between my legs. "Oh, you are soaked," he said as he pulled his hand away and put his fingers into his mouth. He pulled them out, rubbed them on my lips, and brushed my hair away from my face. "I'm going to take a step back so you can take off your dress. Don't be stupid, Zoey. Please don't make me do something I *really* don't want to do to you." He placed his lips beside my ear. "If I have to kill you, I'll fuck every hole, including the ones I make."

I swallowed hard as he took a step back. Closing my eyes, I allowed my dress to drop to the ground, and he kicked it away as soon as I stepped out of it.

My heart pounded against my chest, and the sound it created in my ears deafened me to all other noise in the room. I had no choice but to play his game.

He fisted my hair and dragged me toward the bed. I didn't fight his grip as he threw me onto my back. "I don't need to tie you up, do I?" he asked as he stroked my hair. I shook my head. "Good girl," he whispered.

Anthony unzipped his hoodie and tossed it aside. My eyes wandered over his taut muscles and the tattoos covering his chest as he unbuckled his belt and undid his jeans.

"I want you so goddamn bad." He leaned over and slid my panties down my thighs, making me shiver. "God, you're perfect," he groaned as he drew a deep breath at the sight of my pussy. "Take off your bra." He gestured toward the last piece of material covering my body, and I reached back and unclipped it, sliding it down my arms. I covered my chest with my arms, but he batted them away. "Don't be shy. I've seen it all."

He pulled me toward the edge of the bed by my thighs. His hands raced down my sides, gripping my ass. "I've seen you getting fucked, Zoey. I've seen men do what I want to do to you. It's been torture." He pulled his boxers down and rubbed his cock between my legs. "It doesn't matter now, though. I'll claim your pussy. No one else will ever be able to have you," he whispered before he licked the skin between my breasts. His mouth moved to my nipple and his teeth closed around it, making me flinch. "I want to cause you pain and pleasure." Anthony grabbed his cock and pushed it inside me with a groan that said he needed my pussy more than he needed air. "I'm going to fuck you so good you won't want another man."

He drove his hips into me, fucking me hard and slow at the same time. Each rhythmic, driven thrust went so deep it hurt, yet it made me bite back a moan. I felt guilty for liking it, for wanting more.

His hands never left my skin. He touched every inch of me with fingertips that starved for me. He leaned over and kissed me, biting my lip as he pulled away. "Fuck. I won't last long with you," he said with a hint of sadness. "If I knew I'd be able to have you, I would have been better prepared." He sighed and squeezed the base of his cock as he thrust.

I let my moans escape as he sat up on his hands and

pounded me harder and faster. I almost wanted him to slow down so I could feel him longer. *How sick.* I watched his full lips loosen as low moans rolled past them. His features were so goddamn handsome and rugged, and his cheeks dimpled when he smirked down at me. His amber eyes were intoxicating, causing a clash between my fear and excitement. I reached out and grabbed his sides to hold myself beneath him. He growled as he leaned over, and I felt his weight pressed against me. His hand raced down my sides and grabbed my ass once more. His moan was deep as he came, the slowing of his thrusts leaving me longing for more.

He groaned against my neck before he climbed off and dropped to his knees. He wrapped his hands around my thighs and held me in front of him. His warm breath rolled over my swollen, excited clit, and he buried his face between my legs, licking me as if it wasn't only his hands that had been starving. He'd longed to taste me, and he didn't care that his come was dripping from me. With long strokes of his tongue, he lapped at my wetness, taking every drop of himself with it.

His tongue flicked against my clit and his hands squeezed my hips until my thighs trembled. "I know those moans, Zoey. I know when you're getting close." He growled as he curled his tongue along my clit, burying his face in my pussy as he devoured me.

I gripped his hair as he pushed me over the edge, making me come. I felt guilt and shame for the earth-shattering orgasm he created.

He stood, wiped his mouth, and crawled over me. "You're mine."

My body trembled from the intense orgasm I'd given myself, but a pang of guilt carried over from my fantasy and filled my gut. I shouldn't have come from that—the force and the fear—but the character jumped from the page and into my mind to fuck me senseless. And it wasn't my husband. It was never my husband.

I climbed out of bed and slipped on a pair of fuzzy house shoes. The sound of the door creaking open startled me.

Michael peered into the room. "Someone was busy," he said with a sly grin.

"What do you mean?" I asked with the straightest face I could muster.

"I could hear you moaning from out here."

Oh god, no. In that fantasy state of mind, when I could feel every touch, smell every scent, and hear every filthy word coming from the mouths of those men, I could only *try* to control what I was doing in my real-world body, but I clearly failed that time.

"I . . . ' My cheeks flushed with heat, embarrassed that he'd heard me getting myself off. It was an undeniable need, and I was struggling to keep it in my fantasies any longer. Michael would never fuck me like any of those men, and I *needed* to be fucked like that.

"It's fine, babe," he said as he walked closer, wrapped his arms around me, and pulled me against him. I felt how hard he was beneath his sweatpants.

I bit my lip before dropping to my knees and pulling his pants down. I exposed the beautiful, familiar cock I fell in love with. The one I knew could do so much more to me than it did. I rubbed my hand along the length of him. Yes, he could do *so* much more with that.

I took him into my mouth, and he gripped my hair with a gentle hand. There was no roughness in his grasp. No pain against my scalp. I craved that. I wanted to feel his intense need to shove himself down my throat. There was no rush or uncontrollable thrusts of his hips. No hunger. He merely dropped his head back with a small groan.

I took him to the back of my throat and gagged, creating the sloppy, wet mess that men usually craved. They wanted to see the drool slipping from your lips and down your chin. They loved to know their big cock made you choke. Michael was indifferent to this, although I knew I was making him feel good. He guided my head a bit faster, so I knew he was chasing his pleasure. He deserved it since my panties were soaked with my own come.

"Where do you want me to come?" he asked.

I pulled away from him. "Anywhere you want."

Part of me wanted him to spill his load on my face. The other part of me wanted him to fill my throat.

"Where do you want it?" he asked.

For fuck's sake. Fucking indecisiveness.

"Just come in my mouth," I said with a huff.

He didn't notice.

I took him into my mouth again and sucked him until he guided my head deeper and finished at the back of my throat. I wiped my mouth as I stood, and he wrapped his arms around me again and kissed me.

"Do you want me to take care of you?" he asked, flashing his dark eyes at me.

"No, I'm good." I didn't want to be asked. I just wanted to be taken care of. Just grab me and do it. Even when we were both pleased, I was still on edge about our sex life. I wanted more. I wanted something different. I wanted everything.

Chapter Five

"Yeah, yeah, I know. Dinner at six for Mom's birthday next week. I've had it on the calendar since you mentioned it last time," I told my brother Mark as I jotted down the time and place. I was absolutely pitiful at keeping up with events in my real life. Reality and fiction blurred too often, but I wasn't as "unreliable" as my brother claimed. I was just . . . lost in my own mind.

Anna wasn't *my* mom, but she was an excellent stepmother and deserved that birthday dinner. Mark also wasn't my biological brother. My mother died and my father remarried a woman with a son.

It always felt weird to call Mark my brother once we became adults and moved from beneath the same roof. The feelings of sibling familiarity drifted further away the longer we were apart, but the moment I saw him whenever we got back together, all the memories of Christmas mornings and all the trouble we got into as kids rushed back to me and reminded me that he was my brother regardless of the distance.

That's why the next book made me anxious. A forbidden stepbrother romance. It hit pretty close to home, but it was a trope I was desperate to try, even if I was certain I wouldn't like it. I wanted to wrap myself in the blanket of a taboo fantasy. I wanted to feel the tug of doing something wrong when it felt so damn right.

I lifted the book. The young, shirtless, tattooed man on the cover intrigued me. Curiosity outweighed the guilt I felt for reading the story after getting off the phone with my stepbrother, and I couldn't wait any longer to rip into that fantasy.

I took the book to the couch, cracked open the cover, and began to read. While Michael busied himself with the yardwork he loved, I would disappear into a new, exciting world. The curl in my lip shifted to a tilt of my head and then a rise in my eyebrow. Discomfort became comfortable in ways I never expected—ways that made me feel emotions from every direction. I separated my life from the one on the page and let myself slip into the land of taboo romance.

The doorbell rang and I threw the towel onto the counter with a frustrated breath that forced the hair off my forehead. I'd been volun-told to host Thanksgiving this year, and I was the worst cook. The last thing I needed was for my father and his wife to arrive early and see my disaster, giving my stepmother a reason to take over my kitchen. In retrospect, maybe it wouldn't be so bad if Martha handled it because I sure as fuck didn't want to. It meant cleaning the house from top to bottom, cooking dishes and sides and desserts until my feet and back hurt, and forcing a smile until the last guest left. Then I'd have to clean all over again.

I ripped the oven mitt from my hand and went to the door. When I saw the peek of wavy blond hair through the window, a long exhale showcased my relief. Theo had arrived to save the day. I tugged open the door and met his big smile with a hug.

"Zoey," he cooed. He was younger than me—tall and strong—and when my brown eyes met his blue eyes, it reminded me we weren't biologically related.

"Where's Allison?" I looked behind him for his fiancé, expecting the blonde pixie cut to pop up at any moment.

Theo pulled out of my grasp and held my arms. "We broke up a little while ago."

"Why didn't you tell me?"

"I hoped we'd get back together. Didn't want to start drama for nothing."

I sighed. "Her loss."

It was true. Theo was only twenty, but he ran a successful startup company and already made more money than me. It made me a bit insecure that I was in my twenties and living in a shitty apartment when he could probably pay cash for a house by now, but Theo deserved the world. He'd worked hard, and I didn't begrudge him his success.

"Are Mom and your dad here yet?" he asked as he looked beyond me.

"Not yet, thank fuck," I said as I stepped aside and let him in.

Theo hung his jacket and walked into the kitchen. He glanced around with a disappointed look on his face. Yeah, I had colossally failed at Thanksgiving based on his expression.

"I'm fucking trying, Theo," I snapped before he could say anything.

"You need to chill, Zoey. I think I've arrived just in time to help you relax a bit." He tugged a plastic bag from his pocket.

I cocked my head. "What are those?"

"Edibles. Should get us through this holiday."

I laughed and waved him off. "I have wine, which should also help us get through this family dinner."

"Done and done," Theo said as he handed me a gummy bear.

I rolled it between my fingers before eating it. As he popped two into his mouth, I grabbed the wine from the fridge and poured the crimson liquid into two glasses.

By the time the oven timer rang out, we were a bottle deep and the edibles had kicked in. The heaviness of the day lifted, and it didn't matter that the food would be shitty. It didn't matter that our parents would soon arrive. It only mattered that Theo and I were together again.

I moved out at his age, which meant I left him when he was still a teenage boy. Theo grew up and went on to college, giving up school soon after his business took off.

He became more of a stranger with every holiday and family dinner I came home for, and soon he had a girlfriend who was now his fiancé. Well, *was* his fiancé. His life moved forward while mine remained stagnant. Not even the edibles helped with the dread of the lonely apartment.

"What's the matter?" Theo asked, his big blue eyes sparkling as he sat at the island and snacked on cheese and crackers.

"What happened to you and Allison?" I changed the subject because my thoughts were bringing down my high.

"Don't ask me that," he said with a shake of his head. "It's embarrassing." He popped another cheese square into his mouth and dropped his gaze.

"We've been through some embarrassing shit."

Theo shook his head, his blond hair brushing his fore-head. "Not like this."

I put my hands on my hips and gave him the face I used when we were younger and he'd stolen something from me and I just wanted to hear him admit it. That's all I wanted.

He rolled his eyes. "Fine. She said I couldn't make her come if her clit was the size of the cell phone I never put down. Something like that."

My jaw dropped. "Harsh," I whispered. The edible took over and I accidentally let a hearty laugh follow the word.

He stared at me as I doubled over and couldn't stop laughing. His lips tightened but soon drew into a smile and before long, he was laughing too.

"Fuck off, Zo," he said through his laughter. "It's not funny!"

"It's kind of funny." I forced myself to sober. "I'm sorry, you're right. It's not. I just don't believe it for a moment. Sounds like an excuse to leave." I poured myself another drink and sat beside him.

"It's not. She was impossible to get off. Or I sucked. Either way, no one was happy."

I stared at my glass as I thought about the time I saw Theo masturbating to a picture of me when we were younger. I never thought much of it because you can't put two hormone-filled teens together and not expect at least some weirdness sometimes. I'd snuck a look before I ripped my gaze away, and I saw what he had in his hand before I averted my eyes. He'd have no issue pleasing a woman. So yeah, I still didn't believe her excuse.

"What do you think?" His voice pulled me from my memories. I'd missed the rest of the conversation.

"About what? Sorry," I said.

His eyebrows furrowed. "What were you thinking about?"

"Nothing," I said much too quickly.

"Tell me."

"Absolutely not."

Theo stood and put his hands on his hips, throwing me the same judgmental glare I'd given him moments before. Maybe it was the drugs or the alcohol, but I decided to answer him.

"Fine," I said. "I was thinking about how I caught you choking your chicken when we were younger."

"You saw?" His mouth gaped and he let out a laugh. "Oh god, that's horrifying."

"Well, that's why I think she was lying," I said in a matter-of-fact tone.

As he sat quietly for a moment, a sly smile eased onto his face. "Can I admit something to you, and hopefully we won't remember it tomorrow?"

I nodded. "You know you can."

"I had the hots for you when we were growing up. Then you moved out and I didn't know what the hell to do with myself. So I dated Allison." His cheeks flushed red.

"She was your consolation prize?"

"Well, I sure couldn't have you, Zo. You're my sister."

"Stepsister."

"Same thing." We went silent as I chugged my drink and he stared into his. "I shouldn't have said anything," he whispered as his finger swirled around the rim of his glass.

"If it makes you feel any better, I didn't always consider you the annoying little brother I never asked for."

The oven timer blared and broke the silence between us. As I checked the food and basted the bird with more butter, the heat from the oven toasted my cheeks. When I turned around, Theo was staring at me.

He cleared his throat before speaking. "What if we made it more weird? And then definitely forgot about it tomorrow?"

"What are you asking?" I thought I knew what he

was asking, but it was fucking insane, and I needed to make sure.

Theo stood and walked toward me, cornering me in the kitchen. The heat of the stove warmed my left side, and I felt the lip of the countertop stab into my lower back. I'd never seen his eyes such an intense blue.

"What if we fucked?" His hand wrapped around the back of my neck and the heat of his palm burned me more than the stove.

I swallowed hard. "Theo . . ." I shook my head. "We can't do that."

"Why not, Zo? We're adults now." I watched his full lips move as he spoke.

"Because you're my little fucking brother."

He smiled and bit his lower lip. "It's a title, Zo, like when you call your supervisor your boss."

"When I leave my job, my boss isn't my boss anymore. When I left home, you were still my brother."

"Then I'm your brother. But there's no blood between us, only history. Legal? Perfectly. Ethical? Maybe not. But I'm okay with being unethical today." He drew me closer to his mouth. When he spoke again, his breath brushed my lips. "I'm not asking you to marry me, Zo. That'd be fucking weird. I'm just asking for one time with you. Fulfill this little fantasy of mine, because I think it's yours too."

He was so close I could taste the warm hint of wine dancing across his tongue. He was right. I'd thought about what it'd be like more than once, especially over the last year. Pretty much as soon as he started dating Allison, I felt a sense of jealousy I hadn't expected.

Theo leaned in and kissed me. His lips met mine and he tasted like candy. His hands lifted to my face and his kiss deepened. I let it happen, lost in the feelings circling through my body before a thought crossed my mind.

I pulled back. "Just don't call me your sister while this is happening."

"Will you call me your brother, though?" He forced his gaze into mine.

"Really?"

He rubbed the front of his slacks. "It may or may not be part of that little fantasy I told you about."

Theo dragged me toward my bedroom. He knew where it was because we'd lain in that bed and talked for hours before, but when he pushed me onto the mattress, it took on a whole new meaning. It wasn't a friendly conversation with the person who understood what it was like to deal with our parents. It was fiery and wrong. So fucking wrong.

I blamed the alcohol and the drugs for my hands unfastening the button of his pants and lowering the zipper. He batted my fingers away and crawled between my legs to kiss me. His hands hooked the waistband of my pants and tugged them down my thighs. A growl roared from his throat as he pulled them off and rubbed a hand over my panties. His strong, sure touch made my stomach tighten.

The moment he pulled out his cock, the guilt overtook me and suffocated me. "We can't do this, Theo." I shook my head.

When he wrapped his hand around his dick, it brought me back to the first time I saw it. I didn't see him like that now. The handsome features on his face some-times choked me from across the table at family dinners, and I'd spit my drink out like a teenager. Somewhere along the line, he'd developed the perfect appearance I chased and struggled to find. The cut of his jaw had deepened with maturity. The once thin and ropy muscles had blossomed into hills and valleys of visual pleasure. His eyes held a need for more than a picture of me. He wanted all of me.

Theo leaned over me until his lips found the curve of my neck. "Too late to turn back, Zo. I need to feel you."

He kissed my chest and helped me out of my shirt and bra so he could get his mouth on me again. His tongue swirled around my nipple and sent goosebumps along my skin. Everything in me told me how wrong it was, that we should stop.

But I didn't want to.

"God, you're perfection," he whispered as he kissed down my stomach.

When his mouth reached the waistband of my panties, I gripped his hair and tried to pull him back up. "You're my brother, Theo," I said as I tried one last time to stop us, incidentally saying the one thing he needed to hear that would drive him wild.

"Yes, Zo. I fucking am," he growled as he tugged my panties aside and buried his tongue in my pussy.

My chest rose from the mattress as he licked me in long strokes. He moved his tongue in ways that seemed special, as if he'd spent years memorizing the contours of my body. He probably had.

I gasped as he pushed his fingers inside me, and I

buried my hands in his hair once more. Not to stop him, but to pull him closer. I bucked my hips against his face. *Allison was a goddamn liar,* I thought as my skin pebbled with goosebumps and a shiver rode through every cell of my body. If she couldn't come from this, she was the broken one. Theo reached down and stroked his cock. I moaned much too loudly and tried to cover my mouth to silence my sounds. My chest heaved in pleasure.

He stopped licking and just looked at me, his chin covered in my arousal. "Come for me." He buried his face in me once more, and I writhed against his mouth until I experienced a full-body orgasm that could only come from doing something so fucking wrong.

When I stopped spasming, he wiped his mouth and kissed me. He stroked his dick against my lower belly as I tugged my panties off.

"You know what I want you to do," he said as he playfully wound his hand through my hair.

He lay on the bed and I crawled between his legs. I looked up at him, and he bit his lip in stifled frustration. I hoped I was living up to his fantasy. He was beyond mine.

I took his cock in my hand and stroked him. He groaned as he dropped his head back for a moment before the need to look at me overtook him. I wrapped my mouth around him and took him to the back of my throat. The moans that came from his mouth as I sucked his dick made me drip down my thighs.

"Whose cock are you sucking?" he asked as he balled my hair in his fist.

I pulled back, drool dripping down my chin. "My brother's."

"Good fucking girl, Zo," he moaned. He suddenly stopped me, tugging me away and rubbing a thumb along my lower lip. "I don't want to come in your mouth."

Theo pulled me up his body and planted me on his lap. I grinded against the length of his dick, coating him with my come. His hands rode up my body, his eyes dark and focused on my chest.

"You are so beautiful, and it's not fucking fair that our parents got married." His hand brushed my neck. "Lean back, Zo. I want to see you put me inside you."

I did as he told me. I leaned back and balanced one hand on his thigh as I gripped his cock and slid his head back from my slit. I eased myself onto him as his fingers dug into my hips to make me go slower. My eyes closed as I felt the full length of him inside me, taking up every space he could fill. He felt incredible. The growl that left his lips as I started to move on him told me that I felt incredible to him too. He wrapped his arms around the small of my back and pulled me closer until my chest pressed against his. He kissed me as I grinded on him. I moaned and he absorbed all my sounds into his perfect mouth.

"Are you gonna come again?"

I nodded as I kept riding his dick, grinding my clit against his pelvis. I moaned again and dropped my head against his neck, fighting the spasms of my body.

"You tightening like that is going to make me come," he groaned and rubbed a firm hand down my spine.

"Come for me, Theo," I moaned as his hips stuttered against mine.

"You sure?" he asked.

"Yes, fill me," I moaned.

Theo growled as he came, and I rocked on his raised hips until I did as well. The smell of smoke wafted into the room, and I remembered the dinner. I enjoyed the pleasure for as long as I could before the alarm blared and forced us out of bed.

"Fuck, Zo," he sighed as he got dressed, my come staining the front of his slacks. He tried to brush it off the best he could.

He walked over to me as I stumbled to put on my pants. His lips met mine a final time, and I basked in his touch for a few moments longer.

I drew away from him. "Yeah, Allison's a fucking liar."

Guilt filled me as I came from this story. That wouldn't be my last taboo book. It was a twisted and slippery slope to the darkest side, and I was happy to go along for the ride. No, it didn't make me want to fuck my stepbrother, but I loved how the wrongness turned me on. If I read this to my husband, he'd think I was crazy and lock me away from Mark forever. But I only wanted Michael. I wanted him to fuck me in a way that felt as wrong as this story.

Chapter Six

Michael was working evenings again, and I had the house to myself. I had blazed through my new books, except for one, and I had intentionally saved that book for tonight. The mafia romance. I was most excited to get lost in this particular book, and I already dripped with excitement over my next set coming in the mail. What adventures would they take me on? And with whom? What kind of sick, twisty desires could I play with? I wanted someone strong, bossy, and selfish who saw me as nothing more than a plaything. I wanted to be inconsequential. It shouldn't matter what I wanted or how I wanted it. It only mattered that I was a place for him to spill his come.

While those were the men I liked to read and fantasize about, that wasn't the kind of man I wanted in real life. I had what I wanted. The type of man who helped with dinner and did the dishes after. A man who asked what kind of movie I wanted to watch or how my day went. That was the best kind of man, even if my body desired the alpha assholes portrayed in those stories. My head and heart had never been on the same page. It was more like they were reading two different books that were probably written in two different languages. This was why I anticipated the moments when I could travel to the worlds in my mind—places where I could do whatever and *who*ever I wanted.

There were no repercussions as they came inside me. I didn't have to push a man into the closet to hide him from my husband. I only had to worry about being fucked all the right ways before I returned to the real world. My world was not a fairy tale. It wasn't a dark romance novel. We existed in a cozy, small-town romance novel where the love scenes mostly faded to black. But it was comfortable.

I traced the dark cover, hovering over the well-dressed man clad in an expensive suit. Beneath the fabric waited a man so muscled and handsome it was hard to believe he existed in the real world. The man on the cover didn't merely live in the fantasy realm for all of us bored housewives. That person was somewhere, walking around and fucking women while looking like *that*. I let out a frustrated groan.

Michael didn't have a bad body. He was soft and round, but I still found him extremely attractive, and in some ways, even more so. If I could just unleash the animal locked away in the goddamn escape-proof room deep inside him, he'd be perfect. We'd be perfect.

The title showcased a deep purple font, my favorite color. Red would have been a better fit, but purple on the cover was this author's "thing." I'd read enough of her books to spot her secret.

I wrapped a blanket around myself and began to read, drifting into the hostility of the mafia lifestyle. There was a finesse in the men I didn't see anywhere else. An acceptance of brutality and murder. To have the hand of a man who could fuck you like no other around your throat. A man who had used that same hand to fire a bullet into the head of another man hours earlier. A firm touch that reminded you what he's capable of. That he could kill you if he didn't love to fuck you as much as he did.

I'd have allowed all of it.

I stared at my family, bound and gagged in a big building by the docks. The salt of the sea had ripped holes through the rusted metal, letting the sunlight through to crawl along the concrete floor. My father's eyes widened as he thrashed against the ropes, tossing his thin gray hair over his forehead. My heart broke. None of this was supposed to happen. I fucked up. I should have been the one bound and gagged for my transgressions, not my family, but those motherfuckers were ruthless. This particular family had a reputation as the worst to work with, and I should have considered that. Sometimes desperation made you ask a favor of the devil and his spawn.

"Zoey, you sure took your sweet ass time getting here. I was just about to put a bullet through each of them out of principle," came a low voice from behind me. The grittiness of his tone sent a painful shiver down my spine, yet it nestled into my pelvis. "I don't like to have my time wasted."

While gnawing at the inside of my lower lip, I turned to face Enzo. He had dark hair and tanned skin, which was what I expected of an Italian man like him. What I didn't expect was the ice in his eyes—a bright blue that contradicted every dark part of his appearance.

"Let my family go." I stared him down, my hip cocked. "Your issue is with me, not them!"

Enzo stepped forward, towering over me. "Those fuckers share your blood, which makes them a problem. Do you know how much money you cost me? I lost an entire shipment because of you." His breath rolled over mine, smelling like tobacco and mint. "That pretty fuckin' face of yours ain't gonna save you." His jaw clenched and his lips drew into a tight line.

I swallowed hard. His partially unbuttoned deep-purple dress shirt exposed a ribbed sleeveless t-shirt, and his tattoos peeked from beneath the fabric. Part of me longed to rip it open to see what else was hiding underneath.

Instead, I bit my tongue and lowered my gaze. "I'm sorry."

"There's no apologizing, babygirl." His lips pouted before a grin crept across his face. He looked over at my family, still on their knees, then back at me. "How 'bout this . . ." Enzo stepped into me and grabbed my chin with a rough grasp. I gasped at his touch. "If you let me do anything I want to your body"—his eyes roved downward —"I will consider letting them go."

"Consider?" I gritted my teeth. "I'm not letting you do anything to me for a fucking consideration."

Enzo laughed with a hint of the devil lingering in his voice. "It's cute you think you can *let* me do anything." He reached beneath my dress with a rough touch. "I can take you whether you want it or not, but I can assure you with utmost certainty that you will bury your entire family with your pussy still sore from what I will do to you." He offered a sadistic smile.

Fuck you! And fuck your entire family! I wanted to yell the words toward him, but I screamed them in my mind instead. Even if he killed me and my family, he would sleep soundly that night and nothing I said would make an ounce of difference. When there was money on the line, that family stopped at nothing to come out on top. One way or another.

"Fine," I whispered.

He cocked his head and grinned, cupping his ear. "What was that?"

"Fine! I said fine!" He may have been a cruel and barbaric man, but there was no denying his panty-melting looks. Even though there were worse people to sleep with, my lip curled with a deep-seated disgust.

"Attagirl," he said as he wiped his chin and smirked.

That was the look.

My father writhed against the restraints, trying to scream past the gag in his mouth. One of the men beside him punched him in the stomach, making him curl into himself and fall forward. He panted against the cloth in his mouth as if he was suffocating.

"Go on, tell your pops," Enzo said as he gestured toward my father.

I looked at him with wide eyes. My father clearly heard our seedy agreement, so I saw no reason to repeat it. "I—"

"Now!" he commanded. "Go tell your pops that you will be having your pussy ripped open by me tonight."

I shook my head. "I can't."

He fisted my hair and dragged me toward my father as I fought against his grasp. With his hand still pulling at my scalp, he pushed his arm forward and forced my head closer to my father, who spoke wordlessly against the cloth in his mouth.

"Tell him. Tell him whose cock you'll be choking on tonight." His words were gritty as he fought my attempts to pull away from him.

Tears slipped past my cheeks and dripped onto the weathered concrete beneath me. He pulled me up by my hair and jerked my head back. With a frustrated motion, he drew a revolver and put the cold metal against my head. My father thrashed as he tried to rise to his knees.

Enzo clenched his jaw. "I'm not going to ask again. I swear on my fucking mother . . ." He cocked the hammer without finishing his sentence because he knew I knew what he meant. He didn't need words to tell me he would blow my brains out all over this floor and my father. I could see it in his face and in the surety of his hand around the grip of the gun. He'd do it in half a heartbeat.

"Daddy, I won't be home tonight, because . . ." I leaned down and fought back more tears. I shook my head before speaking again. "I won't be home tonight because Enzo will be fucking me."

"And?" Enzo said with a laugh.

"And he will make me choke on his cock," I rushed out. Heat blazed into my cheeks, and I looked above my father s head because I couldn't bear to look in his eyes.

"Good girl," Enzo whispered as he pulled me away from my father. He rubbed his finger along my trembling lower lip. "Let's go."

He shoved me forward, and I looked back at my father with an ache in my heart. My father caught my eye and started to rise again, but I shook my head. I had made my decision, and I wouldn't let him die trying to save me. I had to do what I had to do to keep them safe, especially since it was my fault they were tied up right now.

I turned my fierce gaze toward Enzo. "Tell your men not to hurt them. I'm giving you what you want."

At first his only response was a taunting smile. He rubbed his chin for a moment before turning back toward his men. "Don't put your hands on them. If I call, kill them."

He shoved me forward again and we got into his BMW. With a groan, I slid into the passenger seat, crossing my legs as my skirt rode up my thighs. The rich leather stuck to the sweat on my skin and pulled with each movement I made to adjust myself.

"Let's get it over with," I said.

Enzo leaned over, his warm breath making goose-bumps rise on my chest. "Don't rush this moment." He looked out the window for a second, then back at me, his eyes flashing blue. He forced my legs apart and dug his fingers into the flesh of my upper thigh. His hand slid further until it rubbed against my panties. "Pretty soon, you'll be *begging* me to stop."

Enzo kept his hand on my thigh as we drove toward his home. My mind raced with fear, anxiety, and a bit of excitement. For a moment I forgot that it wasn't what I wanted. I hated him. I despised him. But my body fucking wanted him. I hoped his threats weren't empty, because I needed to be filled. There were worse ways to settle a debt.

My eyes widened when we pulled into the driveway leading to a towering mansion with archways and extravagant Venetian windows. Ostentatious topiaries shaped into perfect cones lined the driveway. The stone masonry on the mansion's outer shell looked like something out of a magazine. How much money did these people have?

Enzo drove past the house and parked in front of a smaller, simpler building with massive windows that allowed me to see the expansive pool inside. He got out of the car and patted the hood, glaring at me with squinted eyes as his other hand hovered over the revolver on his hip. He gestured toward the front door of the building with a jerk of his head. With a groan, I got out of the car and walked toward him. Gravel crunched beneath my heels. I faced him and crossed my arms over my chest.

He smirked at me and brushed his hand through his thick, dark hair. "Get your ass inside, and you better not have panties on by the time I get there."

With one more encouraging shove, I walked toward the front door, looking back at him as I grabbed the handle and pulled it open. He leaned against the car and watched me, a sly grin on his face. As I entered the building, the smell of chlorine wrapped around me. I walked along the edge of the huge pool and allowed my nose to adjust to the strong scent. The surface of the blue water rippled, and steam rose like translucent ribbons from a jacuzzi beside the pool.

I remembered Enzo's demand to remove my panties before he joined me, so I lifted my skirt and hooked my fingers into the waistband. I pulled them down my thighs and dropped them to my feet, letting the hem of my skirt drop as I squatted to pick them up.

"Damn," said a voice behind me. "I didn't expect you to listen." His strong arms encased my waist and made me stand straight again. He grabbed my panties from my hand, rubbing his fingers along the lace. "Pretty wet for someone who doesn't want it," he said with a rise in his eyebrow.

"Oh, fuck off." I scoffed.

Enzo growled and pulled me into him. He rubbed his hand down my side, his fingers trailing over the bunched fabric of my dress. His hand slithered down my ass and my outer thighs.

"Are you patting me down? Really?"

"Nah." He smirked before gripping my skirt and lifting it toward my hips. He exposed the garter holster that kept my pocket pistol pressed against the skin of my outer thigh. "I already knew you were carrying." He drew the pistol from its holster, took out the magazine, and racked it, ejecting the round in the chamber. His hand hovered over the weapon as he placed it on the glass table beside us. "Just in case you get any ideas," he said as he wiggled the magazine before slipping it into the back pocket of his dress pants.

Enzo walked into me until I felt the cold glass window behind me. The entire wall was made of windows which overlooked the courtyard by the house. My breath caught in my throat as he pressed his body against mine. He drew his pistol and cocked it before pressing it to my temple. He dragged it down until the barrel grazed my lower lip, pulling it into a pout. I could smell the scent of gun oil.

Enzo reached behind me and grasped the clasp on the zipper of my dress. He eased it down, his fingers grazing my back as he lowered the metal down its track. The straps over my shoulders dropped down my arms and sent the dress falling toward the ground. I kicked it away when it puddled around my feet. His breath rolled over mine again as he reached back to unclip my bra. He hooked the barrel of his revolver under the shoulder strap, pulled the bra away and discarding it with my dress. I fought the urge to cover my breasts, feeling anxious with the sun setting behind my exposed body. Landscapers shuffled around the house adjacent to the building, and the wall of windows put me on display.

I gasped as he gripped the revolver again and dragged the barrel further down, dipping between my breasts and rubbing the sensitive skin. His other hand grabbed the flesh of one of them, and I bit the inside of my lip to avoid moaning at his rough touch. He pulled the pistol away for a moment, but the adrenaline continued to course through me. A moan finally slipped out of me as he shoved the barrel of the revolver between my legs. The cold metal pressed into me, rubbing back and forth against my clit.

"You want this, don't you?" he asked with a seductive grin. His free hand grabbed mine and rubbed it over the front of his pants. I nodded quicker than I meant to, and Enzo groaned. "Unbutton my pants," he commanded.

I worked the button loose and lowered the zipper. The fabric spread and exposed his boxers, tented by his girth. As Enzo pulled his boxers down and revealed his full length, my eyes widened at the sight. *That is the most beautiful cock I've ever seen. Why does it have to belong to such a horrible person?*

Enzo pulled the barrel through the excited mess between my legs and drew it away from me. It glistened with my wetness as he brought it toward my mouth. "Clean it off," he said as he maneuvered the barrel until it was vertical against my lips.

I hesitated for a moment before putting my tongue against the metal and licking upward. The curve of my tongue wrapped around the barrel, tasting the mixture of sweetness and metallic electricity.

"Goddamn it, Zoey. I need that perfect mouth on me." He put a strong hand on my shoulder and gripped, pushing me until my knees met rough tile. He grabbed my hair in a fist. "But if you bite me, so help me God . . ." He tapped my forehead with the barrel. "Do you understand?"

I nodded.

"Tell me you understand."

"I won't bite you."

With his hand still wrestling within a ball of my hair,

he pulled my face toward his cock. Heat radiated off his skin, and the scents of cologne and a sweet, pleasant sweat mingled. I reached up and wrapped my fingers around him. He took up my whole hand. His skin was warm, and the head of his cock glistened with his own pre-cum. Enzo grew impatient and shoved himself into my mouth. My conscience got to me the moment he was on top of my tongue, and I gagged as the hard flesh moved within my mouth. He tasted incredible, but it only veiled the man beneath it.

Evil.

Sadistic.

Fucking beautiful.

Damn it.

The moment I gagged, he pulled my mouth away and smacked my cheek. He ran his finger along my lips, wiping at the saliva that had dripped down my chin. "Can we not handle it? You hardly had me in your mouth." He rubbed my lower lip. "I think I'll go make a quick call," he said with an evil grin.

"I can handle that just fine," I said through gritted teeth.

"Then handle it."

I rolled my eyes before taking him into my mouth again. I used my hand to compensate for the length I couldn't take. My hand swirled rhythmically as it moved in sync with my mouth, but that wasn't what he wanted. He grabbed my wrist and pulled my hand away so he could jam himself further into me. I felt him at the back of my throat as he thrust against my face, growling as he fucked my mouth. I gagged and my eyes welled with tears, but he didn't pull away. Instead, he held himself in place until my throat stopped spasming. He pulled out of my mouth, a string of saliva swaying between him and my lips. He smacked my cheek again, making me bite my lip.

"There's no way I'm going to spill my load down your throat. I want it dripping out of your pussy."

I swallowed hard. Part of me was afraid and the other part was . . . intrigued? Enzo unbuttoned his shirt, letting the silk fall off his shoulders and pool at his feet. He kicked it away. The muscles of his abdomen flexed beneath the tight ribbed sleeveless shirt. Ink covered his arms, and I couldn't take my eyes away from an intricate image of a tipped cross with beads hanging from it like a noose.

With a quick motion, Enzo turned me around and pinned me against the cold glass. My breasts pressed against the window. He reached over and grabbed my chin, forcing my face toward the picturesque view outside. "Look," he said with a sultry tone.

I did as he commanded and saw a man in a suit leaning against a pillar at the bottom of a staircase. A cigarette dangled from his relaxed hand, abandoned as his eyes locked on my body.

"Is he just going to watch us?" I asked with a tremble in my tone.

"I hope so. I want him to watch me fuck you," Enzo said as he dragged his hand down my arched back while the other hand popped up my hips.

He rubbed himself between my legs, pressing his heat against me before grabbing my hips and surging inside me. I gasped as he filled me. No amount of my own lubrication could have prepared me for his size. With a forceful thrust of his hips, he pushed himself deeper. I could feel him at the very depths of me, pressing until he couldn't get even a centimeter further. The pain came in waves as he pulled far enough away to come back with a harder slam of his hips. My breasts rubbed against the smooth glass, and the man outside adjusted the front of his pants. I looked away as Enzo pinned me harder, pressing my face against the window. I held back moans despite the intensity. It felt like he was ripping me in two, as he promised he would. The skin between my legs heated up as it begged for a break from the rhythmic, strong thrusts. I bit my lip harder to keep moans at bay as the sound of skin slapping against skin became almost melodic.

"Don't you dare come," he commanded against my ear.

"I won't," I hissed, though I worried he'd make a liar out of me.

An overwhelming feeling of being full engulfed me, and I reached my hand back and put it on his hip. "Time out," I said as he stopped.

He throbbed and felt even bigger just resting inside me. He pulled out, his cock dripping with my excitement. "You have one minute." He smirked. "About the time it takes you to get your ass up on one of those tables over there so I can really show you what pain is."

With shaky breaths, I walked to one of the metal tables and pulled myself onto it. The feel of the cold metal beneath my ass caused my skin to prickle. Enzo took his time walking over to me, giving a moment for the throbbing inside me to calm before I took him again. He leaned over and spit on my pussy, and the warm rush of saliva made me jolt. He palmed me as he smeared his spit between my legs. It made me feel like a whore. His whore.

Enzo grabbed the base of his cock, giving it a few long strokes as he stared at me with a hunger my body mimicked. He rubbed himself against me before surging inside my pussy once more. I looked down at him, filling me and spreading me almost to my limits. My back arched with the contrasting feelings of pleasure and pain, and I lay back on the table. He hooked his hands around my thighs and tugged me toward the edge, grinding his hips into me, rubbing against my swollen, sensitive clit. I rocked my hips against him.

"I told you, you can't come," he growled, firmly grasping my hips and immobilizing my movement.

Selfish prick.

I released a frustrated moan as his rhythm increased in tempo and intensity. By now, the pain pretty much stopped existing as a separate entity from the pleasure swirling within me.

He leaned over me, driving me into the table. "I can tell you're going to come," he said with a frustrated furrow of his brows.

"I'm not trying to!" I clenched my teeth.

He gripped himself and pulled out as my spasms nearly became too much for my body to handle. The pressure within me released, and I could hear the sound of liquid saturating the tiles beneath us.

"Well, fuck," Enzo said as he dabbed at the front of

his slacks. "I can't allow shit like this." He leaned over me, and with an annoyed slap of my cheek, he whispered in my ear. "Change of plans. I'll make you come until you're begging me to stop."

He surged back inside me, putting weight on my pelvis as drove into me with deep, quick thrusts. The spasms reappeared almost instantly, and he pulled out in time to let me explode against him, sending more of my come dripping to the floor. He did it again and again until my body was rigid and tense with exhaustion. Even my jaw throbbed from the writhing strain. I put my hand down and blocked my uncomfortably sensitive clit.

"I told you. You're going to come until it hurts," he said as he ripped my hand away.

He leaned into me and grinded his hips instead of thrusting. The circular motion gave me spasms so strong I cried out. The heat and friction rubbed me until I came again, still stuffed with his cock. My body trembled as I tried to push him away, too sensitive to keep going, but he pinned my wrists above my head and continued to grind against me.

"Please, I can't do it anymore," I pleaded. I never thought I'd tap out from orgasms. The pleasure warped into discomfort as it ravished my body and flooded my senses.

"Is that so?" A sly smile crossed his face as he continued to move his hips against mine. "I think by the time I bust, I'll force you to come one more time for me."

Enzo began to thrust again with shallow and quick movements. I sat up and wrapped my arms around his neck to steady my trembling body, and he thrust in a new upward position. Just when I thought there was absolutely nothing left to saturate the ground, he pulled out enough to let a final gush of liquid pour out of me.

"Oh, good girl," he whispered as he pushed deep inside me again.

The sloshing sound of wetness between us intensified. He growled against my shoulder as his thrusts slowed and grew unsteady. His hands gripped my hips roughly as he came.

Enzo stayed inside me until his come began to seep around him. He pulled out and pulled up his boxers. He tossed my dress at me. "Clean it up." He shifted his weight and crossed his arms.

"With this?" I looked at him in disbelief. This dress was one of my favorites, and I didn't enjoy the idea of having it dry cleaned with the proof of my escapade smeared all over the front. I tried to turn the fabric inside out, but he stopped me.

"Ah ah, I want him to see what I did to his daughter," Enzo said as he wiped a hand through the fine hair of his beard. He snatched my dress from my hands and rubbed the front of it between my legs. "Wear my mark proudly when you return home," he said as he threw my dress back at me. "Like a good girl."

My stomach was tight, and my thighs quivered from my orgasm. I clenched them together as I closed the book and bathed in the remnants of a world I could never imagine living within. A seductive place with danger lurking in every corner, where hatred made for better sex. Hate fucking. The buildup of a raw and visceral rage. Despising someone so much that the only way to keep from blowing up was to release that frustration through sex. Enemies to lovers was my fucking favorite because of it. I didn't care how or why they were enemies, I just wanted them to solve their problems by fucking. I wanted them to fuck until they stopped hating each other and realized the explosion of emotions was from love after all.

Explosiveness. That's what I wanted. What I needed. An animalistic, jealous reaction that made nothing else matter besides being inside me and claiming me as their own. I wanted my pussy to be where the beat of a panicked lover's heart could be soothed. I wanted to feel the combustible line between hate and love, two of the most dangerous emotions we could ever have.

I wanted the danger.

Chapter Seven

"Hey," Michael said with a grin as I walked in the front door.

"Why are you in such a good mood?" I asked as he pulled me into him for a hug.

He held me at arm's length, a smile still planted on his face. "Guess what?"

I couldn't begin to guess. He was never this happy after a workday. "Just tell me. I'm not a good guesser."

"Fine. We've been invited to a party hosted by one of my company's special clients!"

"And we have to go?" His excitement surprised me. Michael wasn't the party type. Hell, neither was I.

"What? Yes! It's an honor to receive an invite. These gatherings are usually kept a secret."

"Clearly not very well." I tightened my lips in a pinched smile.

"I don't even know what sort of party it is, but I was told we have to wear something nice and we have to leave our phones in the car."

"Leave our phones? That doesn't seem the least bit suspicious to you?"

"Not really. Maybe they'll have drugs or something. You wouldn't want phones with *cameras* if you were throwing that sort of rager."

"Rager? How old are you?" I laughed, making his smile widen.

"Fuck off. You know you want to let loose. When was the last time? Before we got married?"

"I don't need to loosen up." I pawed his hands away. "I had my crazy teenage years already. Actually, they crept into my twenties too."

Michael stared at me with a half-cocked smile. "Well?"

I rolled my eyes. "Fine, we'll go, but if you expect me to snort cocaine off your dick, it's not going to happen."

I ran a flat iron through my hair, straightening the unruly waves. Smokey eyeshadow covered my eyelids, making my dark eyes look sultry and seductive. I longed for the beautiful confidence I tried to portray. This mask I wore wasn't me, but for a moment, I felt like the woman in my fantasies. Sexy and alluring. Wanted.

"Wow, you look amazing," Michael said as he walked into the bathroom. He stopped adjusting his tie and stared at me.

"And you look like you're going to the party to do people's taxes."

Michael looked down at himself. "Too much?"

"Yes, too much. Take the damn jacket off. And the tie."

Michael stripped off the garments until he was down to a maroon dress shirt and slacks. He draped the jacket over his shoulder, and I melted as he brushed his hand through his short golden hair. "Better?" he asked as he made a half-spin.

"Yes, much better."

"Do you need help with that?" He gestured toward the back of my dress, still unzipped along my spine. I nodded. His familiar touch along my skin made me throb.

We gathered our things and headed out the door. We drove for what felt like forever, crawling along winding roads with the sun creeping lower on the horizon. Orange hues exploded across the windshield, making us lower our visors at nearly the same time. Pastures of lush grass sprawled on either side of the car, eventually giving way to thick forests. In the middle of fucking nowhere, we pulled onto a long gravel road that took us through the heart of the woods and up to a house.

My jaw went slack as I looked up at the huge home in front of us. It was basically a mansion, with arches and pillars everywhere I looked. The driveway wrapped around a circular fountain spewing a geyser of lit water into the air.

"Jesus Christ, Michael, they have fountains! We do *not* fit in here."

Michael looked around with a similar expression. "He's a down-to-earth guy, relax. Besides, we could get a fountain if we really wanted one."

I put my hand on his arm. "No thank you. It would be one more thing to mow around."

A man in a suit waited beneath the overhang. Michael pulled up beside him and slowed the car to a stop.

"They have a fucking valet?" I let out a dramatic huff as I unbuckled my seatbelt. "I'm beginning to hope there's drugs here. I'm going to need them."

We got out of the car, handed our keys to the valet, and headed toward the massive double doors. Michael let out a low whistle. "Rich people," he said as he knocked.

"The party is toward the back of the house. Just go right in," the valet said as he closed the car door.

Michael turned the handle and pushed the door. We looked around in awe as we stepped onto pristine marble floors. The click of my heels echoed through the hallway, and my eyes wandered along the walls, admiring the finely engraved wood that seemed to be everywhere—flourishes and designs had been etched into every surface. The dull sound of music drifted toward us from the far end of the hallway. No wonder the guy told us to walk in. No one would've heard us knock.

At the end of the hallway, a spiral staircase led to the lower floor. A nervous sweat collected on my palm as it touched the cool crystal railing. I gave Michael a side-ways glance and he shrugged.

"Michael Edwards, is that you, my friend?" came an excited voice as we reached the end of the stairs.

"Sure is," Michael called back.

"I worried you weren't going to come." A tall figure

came into view, and he brushed his hand through his long, well-kempt hair.

"I wouldn't miss it!" Michael said, feigning excitement. He gave a broad, believable smile as he held out his hand and they greeted each other.

The man turned and set his gorgeous brown eyes on me. "And this must be the lovely Zoey?"

"Sure is. I don't think we've ever met," I said as I held my hand toward him. His hand grasped mine, his skin warm and sweaty.

"I'm Mr. Roderick. That's all you have to worry your pretty little head about." He touched my cheek. "Come, come, follow me."

After exchanging a nervous glance, Michael and I followed Mr. Roderick through his home. He looked too young to possess such an extravagant residence. Generational wealth, maybe? Involved in something illegal, perchance?

He stopped at a door and turned to face us. "Did you leave your phones as requested?"

Michael nodded, and Mr. Roderick led us through the doorway. The music rushed toward us, making my heart thump against my chest. Dim lights cast little more than shadows through the room, but I could see a naked woman lying on an overstuffed white couch, passed out. Her arm draped over her bare torso, just beneath her exposed breasts.

What the hell kind of party is this?

In the corner, a man hovered over another naked woman and sniffed lines of powder off her chest. He inhaled deeply, pulling away long enough to devour the skin of her breasts. She moaned as she sniffed powder from a necklace around her neck. Another pair of people were entwined at the waist, moving together as sweat coated their bodies and reflected the gentle gleam of the overhead lights.

I didn't bother with a sideways glance this time. I stared at Michael with no pretense of subtlety. *What the hell have we gotten ourselves into?* I now understood the reasoning behind the no-phone rule.

A woman across the room leaned against a shiny black piano. Her champagne-colored dress opened across her slim waist, exposing her stomach, and the skirt hugged her hips. She caught me staring, and a flirty smile crossed her face.

"You guys okay?" asked a voice from far away. "Zoey, you okay?" The voice grew closer, and strong hands shook my shoulders. "Zoey!" his voice grew stern.

I escaped my trance as the music grew louder and Mr. Roderick's touch became firmer. "I'm okay, it's fine. Just a bit shell-shocked," I said as I turned to face him. *Not a lie.*

I had been to some fucked-up parties in my lifetime, and what I was seeing wasn't all that shocking comparatively, but it wasn't the same as a married woman. It was different with Michael there because I had to be a different person in his presence. I'd left this sort of wild lifestyle behind when I let him slide the gold band around my finger.

"Do I have to worry about you two being narcs?" Mr. Roderick laughed with an uncomfortable snap at the end.

Michael wrapped his arm around me. "No, don't worry. We don't get invited to parties like this very often."

"Or ever," I said under my breath.

Another man in a suit came by with a fake smile plastered on his face. He held the silver tray in his hand toward me, and I eyed the white baggies. A goddamn display of drugs toted around like they were fucking hors d'oeuvres.

"Pick your poison," Mr. Roderick said with a smile, wrapping his arms around both of us.

I hesitated before grabbing one of the baggies. Michael glanced at me with a pinched face and a frown.

"You guys need to relax," Mr. Roderick said with a smirk. He motioned toward the woman I'd been staring at, and I could somehow hear her footsteps over the music as she came toward me. She touched my arm with soft fingertips.

"Mira, show them to a quiet area where they can decompress," Mr. Roderick said.

"With pleasure," Mira said. She wrapped her arms around our waists and guided us into an adjacent room. Once she'd closed the door, the music faded into a low thump again. She gestured toward the couch, and we all sat down. Mira slipped her heels off and drew her legs up, showing a flash of black between her legs.

"It's a bit much, I know," she said with a smile.

"It's just different," I said.

Mira pulled a baggie of powder from between her full cleavage. "Different is good, no?" She opened the baggie and dumped its contents onto the glass table, splitting it into three even lines before reaching down the front of her dress and pulling out a straw. Her blonde hair slid along the glass as she leaned over and snorted a line. She sat up, wiped her nose, and held the straw toward us.

I reached out and grabbed the straw. "Fuck it," I said as I pulled my hair over my shoulder and snorted the second line. I handed it to Michael and with a quick paw at his arm, he leaned over and sniffed up the third. My sinuses burned, and the drugs lit up my brain like fucking Christmas lights. I draped a leg over Michael's lap and relaxed against the back of the couch.

Mira fanned herself. "This always makes me so overheated."

I knew what she meant. My skin felt warm and pleasant, like I was wrapped in my favorite blanket with a really good book.

"There's a bit more than just coke in there." Mira giggled.

"Like what?" Michael asked as he sat taller. He leaned forward and cocked his head, and his leg started shaking.

"A little bit of this, a little bit of that," she said as she reached behind her neck and untied the top of her dress. The fabric spilled down her body, exposing her full breasts. She lay back with a satisfied sigh.

Michael and I stared at her, admiring the soft curves of her body. If she'd aimed to distract us from the unknown contents of the drugs we'd just inhaled, she'd succeeded.

"I want to kiss you," Mira said with a pout of her lips.
Me?

Before I could answer, she crawled toward me with

intoxicated movements. She snuggled against me before wrapping her hand around my neck and drawing me in for a kiss. Mira's lips were soft and had a hint of alcohol on them. I pulled away to look at Michael, whose eyes were locked on us.

"Can I fuck her?" Mira asked with a slur of her words, her blue eyes meeting Michael's.

His mouth dropped open. He shook his head but his motions turned into a nod, as if he was fighting with himself about what he wanted.

"You can watch," she said with a bite of her lip.

Michael scooted back a little to let me lie back, and Mira pulled my attention back to her with hungry lips. I moaned as she kissed my neck. Her hands lifted my dress as she lowered herself between my legs, and I reached back and rubbed the front of Michael's pants, feeling his twitching erection through his slacks. I gasped as she pulled my panties aside and placed her warm mouth against me. She licked me as if the drugs fueled her tongue. I opened my eyes at the sound of Michael's zipper falling. He pulled out his cock and I stroked him, moving my hand with the motion of her mouth. The more she pleased me and made my back arch in ecstasy, the faster I stroked him. He thrust his hips forward against my touch. Michael's cock throbbed in my hand as a hot and hungry tongue devoured me.

Mira slipped her fingers inside me, fingering me as she licked me. The drugs coursed through my veins, awakening my senses and taking over my nerves like a wildfire. I'd never felt such sensations.

Mira sat up and wiped her mouth with the back of

her hand before licking me off her fingers. "I have an idea. I'm going to go get Mister! Let's turn this threesome into a foursome."

She didn't ask. She *told* us. She stood and left the room without covering herself. I looked at Michael once she was gone.

"Should we?" I asked with heavy breaths.

"I-I don't know. Maybe?" he said with a nervous brush of his hand through his hair.

"Let's see what happens," I whispered to Michael. "We can stop at any time." It was beginning to feel like a scene from one of my novels. I pinched myself to make sure I hadn't fallen asleep while reading, but it was very real.

When Mira returned with Mr. Roderick, he wore a broad smile across his face. "Mira said you guys want to swap?" he asked with a curious lift of his eyebrows.

"Well, I mean . . . we . . . thought about it," I said.

"I can tell you this, Michael. If you fuck Mira, you won't regret it," Mr. Roderick said. He turned his sultry gaze toward me. "And it looks like I wouldn't regret it with her, either."

My heart raced within my chest. He was handsome and his confidence was sexy, but I couldn't imagine this really happening. Michael sleeping with someone else? *Me* sleeping with someone else?

"Shall we, Zoey?" Mira bit her lip.

Mr. Roderick sat on the opposite side of the couch, and Mira grabbed my hand and helped me to my feet. I looked at her with wide eyes. I reached down to slip off my heels, and she smiled sweetly at me. Her hand slid toward my back and lowered the zipper on my dress. The fabric fell past my shoulders, exposing my black bra, and Mira kissed me as she unclasped my bra. I slid it off, along with my dress, and Mira removed her skirt.

I bit my lip as I stared at her body. Only black panties covered her. She hooked her fingers into the waistband of my panties and eased them down, and I kicked them away before doing the same to her.

Mira pushed me onto the couch and straddled my waist, pressing her warmth against my lap. She kissed me, moaning against my mouth as Mr. Roderick reached over and grabbed her ass. Her lips trailed down my neck and over my breasts until her tongue wrapped around my nipples. With an eager hand, she squeezed the flesh of my chest. I reached between her legs and found her wet excitement. I rubbed her, making her moan.

"Can I fuck him?" she asked in a whisper against my mouth as she kissed me again. Her eyes flashed at Michael.

Her question caught me off guard and the thought twisted my stomach into knots, but the way she bit her lip and stared at me—coupled with whatever drugs we'd done—made me nod my head. She slid off my lap and straddled Michael's. He looked at me for permission before he even put his hands on her sides. Despite the sweat forming on my temples, I agreed with a curt nod.

As Mira kissed him, I ached with jealousy, but it wasn't the sort of jealousy that made me feel sick. It turned me on. She grinded herself against his cock as she worked off his pants.

The moment Mira's lips met Michael's, Mr. Roderick

leaned into me for a kiss. He smelled like cologne and liquor, a potent smell that was neither pleasant nor unbearable. His lips spread on mine, and I whimpered as he bit my lower lip. My stomach tightened and a wave of guilt-fueled nausea rushed through me. I had no idea why. Mira had her mouth on Michael's and he seemed fine.

Mr. Roderick pulled away and looked at me. There was a hint of leftover powder around his nostrils. When I didn't stop him, he wrapped a hand around the back of my neck and drew me toward him for another kiss as his hand wandered to my bare thigh. I made a noise that I didn't intend to make. A slightly audible breath of protest.

The moment Michael heard it, he leaned away from Mira and looked at me. I swallowed hard. His eyes remained on me as Mr. Roderick widened his kiss against my mouth. Michael's cheeks flushed red, but the twist in his lips made me sure it wasn't only from arousal. Just by looking at me and witnessing the subtlest change in my body language, he knew I needed *him*, not Mr. Roderick.

"Mira . . . I'm so sorry . . ." He pulled away from her, trying to escape her relentless kisses. "I can't do this."

Mira smiled at him, wiping the lipstick from around her lips. "It's okay." She climbed off his lap and grabbed her dress from the floor. Her cheeks were a deep shade of red that stood out against her pale skin.

Though Mira had listened to Michael, Mr. Roderick didn't stop his hand's ascent up my thighs or pull his mouth from my skin as he dropped to one of my breasts.

"I said I can't do this, Mr. Roderick, which means *she*

can't do this," Michael said, raising his voice with a sternness I'd never really heard.

"Mister . . ." Mira whined.

Mr. Roderick pulled away from me with a frustrated groan, straightened himself, and adjusted the crotch of his pants. "Well, Michael, don't feel rushed to leave. I'm sorry if we offended either of you. I'll see you at our next meeting, okay?"

They left the room, closing the door behind them.

Michael released a slow exhale, probably worried he'd lost his client over what had happened . . . or what hadn't happened. I leaned over to grab my dress, but he snatched it away from me.

"Not yet." Michael dropped my dress to the floor as he stood in front of me, wiping lipstick from around my mouth. His thumb trailed along my lower lip, sending a shiver through me. It was my favorite thing men did in the books I read. That possessive touch that made me certain he was thinking about my mouth on him.

"I can't watch you with another man," Michael said through a clenched jaw. He grabbed my hand and pulled me to my feet. He wrapped his arms around me and inhaled a deep breath as if he'd been preparing for this moment. "I knew what kind of party this was. I wanted to give you a special night. I tried, but I can't do it." His hand eased between my legs, rubbing my slick clit. "You're mine, Zoey. And I know the things you want. I've read parts of the books you read. You think I wouldn't wonder what makes my wife disappear for hours on end? I know you want spontaneity and roughness." Michael fisted my hair and craned my neck.

"You want me to fuck you like I'm not me," he said against my mouth as he leaned in and kissed me. "You want me to push you down." He turned me around and forced me onto my knees on the couch. I held onto the back of it for support. "You want me to spread your legs." He pushed my thighs apart with a rough jerk of his knee. "And you need me to fuck you like I want nothing more than to use you. To hurt you. Like I don't love you."

I gasped as he leaned into me and surged inside me. I was wet as hell, flooding further from the growl within his words, a feral dialect I had never heard in his voice before.

Michael grinded his hips into me, pushing his cock as deep as he could go. He fucked me hungrily, like he wanted nothing more than to unload inside me. He didn't care about rubbing me or making me come. His only focus was holding back my screams as he pounded into me harder than I'd ever felt. He growled against my neck as he slowed his thrusts, pushing deeper into me until I felt like he would burst through me.

"I'm not coming in your pussy, sweet girl." His voice made me melt. "I want to come on your face and in your mouth," he said with a groan.

I froze, shocked by the desire woven through his words. Michael grabbed my arm and dragged me off the couch. He fisted my hair before grabbing my shoulder and forcing me to my knees on the rough floor. He shoved his cock in my mouth, still wet from being inside me. I tasted myself and what his words had done to me. What his touch had done to me. I gagged as he held the back of my head in a firm grasp and pulsed his hips against my face with no inhibition. Carelessly. Selfishly.

"Good girl," he whispered as he dropped his head back. "Such a good fucking girl." He gripped himself and pulled away. "Open your mouth," he commanded. With the way he spoke, I would do just about *anything* he asked me to do. *Anything.*

I spread my lips and stuck out my tongue, looking up at him with big, dark eyes. I watched him rub his cock in long, sensual strokes. His lips parted as he focused on the head of his dick. I stared at his perfect hands as they worked him up to spill his load into my mouth. It was incredible to watch. It was mouthwatering. It made me anticipate every drop.

"Sweet girl," he groaned. I knew he was close. I knew his breathy exhale more than I knew my own signals. He snatched my head back and growled as he came on my tongue and smeared the head of himself against my lips. "Don't swallow yet," he said as I kept my tongue out, enjoying the salty taste of him dripping from the tip. He looked so unlike himself, uninhibited in ways I'd never seen from him. I loved it.

He leaned down and reached into his pocket, tugging out his cellphone. I looked at him with a surprised cock of my eyebrow. Michael was such a rule follower, so I couldn't believe he'd broken the one decree within these walls. With a grin, he turned on the camera and took a picture of me—naked, on my knees, and with his come dripping onto my chest.

Is this really happening right now? Could Michael be fulfilling the most deeply rooted fantasy I've had?

"Swallow, but don't wipe your lips off," he growled. "I want you to keep me on them. I want you to taste me the rest of the night. On the ride home. When we get home. I want you to remember you're mine."

If you want to read more about the Mafia fantasy in this book, check out Lauren's Mafia duet. Start with Edge of Sin: Books2read.com/EdgeofSin

Dark Hitchhiker romance standalones:
Hitched: Books2read.com/Hitched
Along for the Ride: Books2read.com/MFMHitchhiker
Driving my Obsession: Books2read.com/DrivingmyOb
session
Across State Lines: Books2read.com/AcrossStateLines
Don't Stop: Books2read.com/Dont-Stop

Here are some of Lauren's DIET books:
The Slaycation series, a dark romantic comedy series.
Start with Sinners Retreat: Books2read.com/SinnersRe
treat
Morally Grey: Books2read.com/MorallyGrey
Stranger Session: Books2read.com/StrangerSession
Last Mistake: Books2read.com/LastMistake
Protect Me: Books2read.com/ProtectMeNovella
Dark Decisions: Books2read.com/DarkDecisions
Frisky the Snowman: Books2read.com/FriskytheS
nowman

Men of Mayhem and Vengeance: Books2read.com/
MOMAV

If you want darker reads, check out these:
Karma: Books2read.com/KarmaNovella
Unethical: Books2read.com/UnethicalNovella
Wanted: Books2read.com/WantedNovella
Toxic Duet: Books2read.com/Toxic-Love
Captured: Books2read.com/CapturedBook
Never Let Go: Books2read.com/NLG

Connect with Lauren

Check out LaurenBiel.com to sign up for the newsletter and get VIP (free and first) access to Lauren's spicy novellas and other bonus content!

Join the group on Facebook to connect with other fans and to discuss the books with the author. Visit http://www.facebook.com/groups/laurenbieltraumances for more!

Lauren is now on Patreon! Get access to even more content and sneak peeks at upcoming novels. Check it out at www.patreon.com/LaurenBielAuthor to learn more!

Also by Lauren Biel

To view Lauren Biel's complete list of books, visit:

www.LaurenBiel.com

Or

Campsite.bio/LaurenBielAuthor

About the Author

Lauren Biel is an author with several titles in the works. When she's not working, she's writing. When she's not writing, she's spending time with her husband, her friends, or her pets. You might also find her on a horseback trail ride or sitting beside a waterfall in Upstate New York. When reading her work, expect the unexpected.

To be the first to know about her upcoming titles, please visit www.LaurenBiel.com.

www.ingramcontent.com/pod-product-compliance
Lightning Source LLC
Chambersburg PA
CBHW021929170626
46807CB00007B/3042